IN TOO DEEP

ADAM CROFT

GET MORE OF MY BOOKS FREE!

To say thank you for buying this book, I'd like to invite you to my exclusive *VIP Club*, and give you some of my books and short stories for FREE.

To join the club, head to adamcroft.net/vip-club and two free books will be sent to you straight away! And the best thing is it won't cost you a penny — ever.

Adam Croft

For more information, visit my website: adamcroft.net

BOOKS IN THIS SERIES

Books in the Knight and Culverhouse series so far:

1. Too Close for Comfort
2. Guilty as Sin
3. Jack Be Nimble
4. Rough Justice
5. In Too Deep

To find out more about this series and others, please head to adamcroft.net/list.

1

Tanya Henderson let the last drop of red wine fall from the glass onto her tongue, before stopping for a moment to consider whether or not she should open another bottle. It probably wouldn't be a good idea. She knew that a glass or two of wine — and no more — often helped her to think more clearly, to put all of her stresses to one side for a few hours and concentrate on the task in hand. And what a task it was.

Her job as an investigative journalist meant that she was used to having to deal with some real shits. It was her responsibility to dig down into the murkiest depths of criminality and corruption, exposing those people who used their money and their power to create more money and more power. In her time she'd uncovered some big scoops: a billionaire American computer software tycoon who'd been siphoning off money that was being put into a charity foundation and a married Premier League footballer who'd been sleeping his way around half of London and paying off the women to keep them quiet. It wasn't anything that had particularly surprised anyone who'd paid attention to the news stories when they came out: it was an unfortunate fact that most people just accepted this sort of stuff went on.

As much as she loved her job, Tanya got frustrated sometimes at the amount of work that had to go into each investigation, not to mention the depressingly short odds that meant most of them wouldn't end up in a story. More often than not, there just wasn't enough evidence to go on. If people were going to commit a major fraud, they tended to cover their tracks pretty well. But even so, Tanya Henderson was there, ready to pounce on any tiny loophole they managed to leave. It wasn't high turnover 'churn' journalism — she might only have a story published once every couple of years — but she knew that when she did it would make her some big money and give her the satisfaction of exposing some of society's biggest crooks.

And she knew the case she was working on right now could potentially blow a hole in the entire system of local government. It was something that had come to her attention as a local resident, but which she was planning to expose using her position at a national newspaper. The Inquirer didn't have the biggest circulation of all the national newspapers by a long shot, but it enjoyed a steady readership of around 50,000 a day — more when they broke a big story.

The story she was working on right now was going to

have to function a little differently. Locally, she knew the story would be huge, but for a national scandal she was going to have to dig deeper and find other instances of the tentacles of corruption creeping into local government around the country.

A lot of journalists she knew tended to form teams, getting younger, less experienced journalists on board to help gather information, speak to witnesses and generally try to build a bank of evidence from which they could form a story. But for every time that had been successful, Tanya knew of at least five occasions where one of the juniors had majorly fucked up and blown the whole story before it had even begun. That wasn't something she ever wanted to risk. Slowly, slowly, catchy monkey.

Before she could decide whether or not to open another bottle of wine, her mobile phone began to vibrate next to her on the wooden desk. As the phone skidded gently across the surface, she looked down at the bright display. It was a withheld number. Nothing unusual in her line of work. She picked up the phone, swiped her finger across the screen and lifted it to her ear.

'Yep?' she said — her regular greeting. Giving nothing away as usual.

There was silence at the other end of the line. She gave it a few moments before speaking again.

'Hello?'

Tanya heard a light click, and then the phone went dead. She pulled the mobile away from her cheek and looked at the display. It had reverted back to her smartphone's home screen. She was used to getting some abusive phone calls every now and again — it went with the job, and was one of the reasons why she changed her number every few months — but she'd never had a silent call before. She hoped it would be the last, but made a mental note to give her mobile provider a call in the morning, just in case she needed to get her number changed again.

Sighing, she leaned back in her chair. Christ, the mountain of data seemed to be growing by the day. That was one of the downsides to keeping your work to yourself, she realised. Still, it was better than risking the alternative. As she'd come to learn, you couldn't trust anyone but yourself.

She considered calling it a night. It was already gone midnight and her brain was getting to the point where it wasn't going to be doing her much good to stay up any longer. But those files, the gigabytes of documents — deeds, agreements, financial records — all needed going through. And the sooner it got done, the more likely she'd be to have her scoop.

Before she could decide what to do, she heard the faint sound of her doorbell — a soft *bing-bong*, just loud enough for her to hear it from this side of the house but not too loud that it made her jump. When you've got your head stuck into investigating some of the biggest crooks in society, anything can make you jump.

She yawned, locked the screen on her computer, stood up and pushed her desk chair out behind her before making her way through to the hallway. She enjoyed living here. It wasn't a small house by anyone's standards — the kids had plenty of space and Tanya was very grateful to have her own home office — but it seemed a whole lot bigger and emptier when John, her husband, was away with work, as he was this weekend.

As she got to the front door, she could see the blurred figure behind the glass — big, burly, black. But then again, everyone looked that way when they were standing the other side of that front door. It was a trick of the light, the frosting on the glass. Backlit by the glowing orange street-light at the end of the driveway, a five-year-old girl would look menacing from the other side of that door.

Sliding the brass chain across and unlocking the latch on the door, Tanya froze for a moment as it swung open and she registered what was in front of her.

A man — probably — dressed head to toe in black, except for a pair of piercing green eyes that looked at her from two of the holes in his balaclava. The first time she registered the crowbar was when it flashed it front of her eyes, the steel reflecting the light of the streetlamp just before she felt the impact on the side of her skull.

She felt instantly sick, an enormous wave of nausea rising from the pit of her stomach as her brain released a huge surge of adrenaline to deal with the trauma. She staggered to her side, crashing into the door and hearing it clatter against the wall. She felt another blow come down from above, this time on the back of her neck, just above her shoulder blades.

The dizziness grew, beginning to overwhelm her, and

she felt her vision and hearing start to blur and cloud. In the moment before she lost consciousness, she could just about make out the soft, unfocused smudge of white and pink at the top of the stairs and the faint voice that faded away into the distance.

'Mum? Mummy?'

2

The whisky glass was feeling heavier in Jack Culverhouse's hand with every passing minute. He'd seen with his own eyes how many police officers of his age had ended their careers at the bottom of a bottle, but he was determined to stay in control. One drink a night was about all he was having at the moment. Two, perhaps, if it had been a particularly tough day, which it often was.

The dreaded drink had nearly finished his career once already — he had been back in the saddle only a few months since being suspended from Mildenheath CID during a recent double-murder investigation. The killings had shaken the major crimes unit at Mildenheath for a number of reasons. Having happened barely weeks after one of their own, Luke Baxter, had been killed in the cross-fire while apprehending a serial killer, their most recent high-profile case had seen them investigating the murders of two paedophiles. Culverhouse had been of the opinion — and he'd made this known — that whoever had carried out those killings was doing them a favour. The powers-that-be didn't quite agree, leaving him sidelined with only a bottle of brown liquid for company.

He was used to not having people around — that had always been the way since his wife, Helen, had walked out on him all those years ago, taking his daughter with her. But one thing Jack Culverhouse could not live without was his work. That had been his *raison d'être* — the whole reason he got up in the morning. Having that taken away from him had almost finished him off.

Retirement wasn't something he ever considered, although he wasn't far off being able to take his full police pension if he wanted it. He knew some forces tended to pressure officers into retirement after a certain age or a certain number of years' service, and he was grateful that he had Charles Hawes as his Chief Constable — a man who was far too wishy-washy to ever make real waves in policing, but who was far more sympathetic to Jack's style of policing than most people. He knew that when Charles Hawes left his post, it would be the beginning of the end for him.

Jack was old school, and he wasn't afraid to admit it. He'd seen the changes in policing, seen how it had become a glorified office job. He refused to accept the winds of change, though, and carried on regardless in his own way. He was fortunate in that Mildenheath CID had a certain degree of autonomy which a lot of major crimes units didn't. It hadn't been subsumed into a bigger, faceless unit at county — or regional — level and had managed to resist any major reforms for a number of years, much to the chagrin of the county's elected Police and Crime Commissioner, Martin Cummings.

But it wasn't work that was on Jack Culverhouse's mind as he sat in silence, save for the sound of his own heavy breathing, the air whistling through his nostrils as he nursed the crystal glass in his hand. It was Emily. The daughter he hadn't seen for nine and a half years. She'd been three years old at the time her mother had taken her, and now would be getting on for thirteen. It seemed impossible that she would be a teenager in a matter of weeks — that sweet little girl with blonde pigtails, barely waist height, singing nursery rhymes back at him. He tried not to think about it too much. It wasn't doing him any favours.

It wasn't a situation he was ever going to be able to accept or deal with, but it had started to become normal. First of all there was Emily's fourth birthday. Then came the day when they'd been gone a year. Time had blurred, and before he knew it he'd realised that Emily had been gone for longer than she'd been with him. A few years later it was the same milestone with Helen. Looking back now, the time when they were around seemed like a blip on the radar of Jack Culverhouse's wider timeline. And that hurt.

Just as he'd started to come to terms with things and realise that they weren't going to change, Helen had turned up on his doorstep unannounced. That was almost a year ago now, but when he closed his eyes he could still see her face in front of him. The same as he remembered, but older, more tired. Whenever he thought back to happier times — times when she and Emily had both been around — it was that jaded, haggard face that he saw rather than the younger, more vibrant Helen. Try as he might, he couldn't visualise how she used to look.

It wasn't that she'd turned up out of the blue that hurt; it was the fact that it seemed to be for completely no reason whatsoever. She didn't have anything new to tell him — other than the fact that she'd been diagnosed with some sort of mental disorder — and the things that she did tell him turned out to be mostly lies. Like the story about having moved out to Spain, for instance. Jack had quickly been able to find out that was a lie by getting in touch with a police contact in Alicante, who was able to confirm that there had been no record of Helen living in Spain at any point over the past several years.

Even though she'd been as flaky and elusive as ever, he couldn't help but be hurt all over again when she'd left. They hadn't parted on the best of terms, but what was she to expect? You don't just disappear for eight and a half years, turn up out of the blue one day and expect everything to be fine. The problem was that she just couldn't see that. It was as if she'd turned up solely to have a dig at him. No information, no Emily, no nothing.

But he'd done angry. He'd done irate. He'd done exasperated. Now there was only hurt and regret.

Jack, like everyone, had a tipping point when it came to alcohol, where if he drank too much he became irritable and unreasonable — more so than usual, that is. But his recent ration of just one or two glasses of whisky a night had put him regularly in the zone where he became reflective and regretful. And it was a feeling of regret that overwhelmed him as he stared glassy-eyed at the mobile phone on the arm of the sofa. He had a contact number for Helen, the one she'd used last year when she came back on the scene. He knew, however, that it wasn't a permanent number and that in all likelihood she would have already moved on again. Another phone, another country, another life.

In a way, part of him hoped that was the case, and while she didn't necessarily need to hear what he had to say, but he had to say it nonetheless. Although he wanted to let her know how he felt, he still couldn't shake that stubborn alpha-male ego that lay at the core of Jack Culverhouse. Deep down he knew that he was doing this more for himself than anyone else.

He slugged back the last mouthful of whisky, feeling the liquid warming his throat as it slipped down towards his stomach, before picking up the phone and scrolling through the contact list to Helen's last-known number. He looked at it for a moment, then decided to take the plunge.

The few seconds that it took for the call to connect seemed like an age. Then came the words that he had always expected to hear.

'The person you're calling is not available. Please leave a message after the tone. When you have finished leaving your message, please hang up.'

The *beep* seared through Jack's skull, mixing and mingling with the effects of the alcohol. He closed his eyes and swallowed hard, trying to fight back what he knew must come out.

'Helen. It's me. It's Jack.'

3

The young police officer grimaced as he looked down at the perverse shape of the woman's skull. It was dark and cold outside the house, and he shivered as he put his hands back in his pockets, trying to get warm.

The paramedics had arrived just moments before him and his partner, PC Chloe Kirkpatrick, and were now attending to the woman lying on the ground.

'I think we're going to need to radio this one in for CID, Stu,' Chloe said. 'We need an SIO on the scene.'

He knew she was right; they were way out of their depth on this one. Before he could murmur his assent, however, Chloe was already speaking into her radio.

'6224 to Control. I'm at the incident on Manor Way with PC Easton. I think we're looking at a very serious assault. We need a senior investigating officer, over.'

There was a couple of seconds of silence before the reply came back over the radio.

'Received, 6224. Will keep you posted, over.'

The original call had come in from a neighbour of the victim, who had reported that her four-year-old daughter had knocked on his door in the middle of the night to say that her mummy was hurt. When he came out to see what the matter was, he found the woman lying on her front doorstep with her head caved in. Somehow, though, she was still alive. The officer didn't need a paramedic to tell him that — he could hear the low, guttural noise that came from the woman's throat, a cross between a growling dog and a train screeching to a halt.

The noise made him feel sick to the pit of his stomach; seeing people in this sort of state was something he wasn't sure he could ever get used to. This was one of the reasons he knew that he didn't want to go into CID. After all, the Criminal Investigation Department was the team who were tasked with investigating murders, rapes, and other serious violent crimes. His squeamishness tended to put Traffic out of the equation too, unfortunately. Sometimes he wished he'd just got a job working in a shop somewhere. It would be a lot easier.

'What do we know?' he asked the two paramedics, both of whom were busy trying to assess the situation. Stu knew that putting his brain into work mode was the only way he was going to be able to keep hold of his stomach.

'Blunt trauma to the skull, by the looks of things,' the paramedic replied. 'It's made a mess of this side of her head, and it looks as though she's been hit on her upper back, too. There's some bruising starting to appear already.'

'What about moving her?' he asked. He was conscious of not wanting to get in the way, but having only been in the job a few months, he was keen to pick up all he could.

'That's always the difficult decision,' the older paramedic answered, throwing a glance at his partner that said *Is this guy for real?* 'In this case, she's still breathing and we've got a pretty decent pulse. She needs urgent treatment, and she's not going to get it here.'

'Right. Is there anything we can do?'

The older paramedic decided to leave it to his partner to answer this one.

'Just try and keep a bit of distance, give us a bit of space. You'll need to keep this lot away, too,' he said, gesturing towards the small crowd of neighbours who'd come out in their dressing gowns and slippers to see what was going on. Right down the road, curtains were twitching and lights were coming on in bedrooms.

'I'll do it,' Chloe said, heading off towards the end of the drive. Although she was barely five and a half feet tall and was invisible if she turned sideways, PC Kirkpatrick took no prisoners when she was trying to get people to do as she asked. She'd been known to take down men twice her size in under a second. The neighbours seemed to pick up that vibe, too, as they mostly made their way back to their respective homes, with just a few stragglers insisting on trying to get a good view of what was going on.

It was at times like this that Stu despaired of the Great British public. What on earth possessed people to want to stop and look at something like this? He'd lost count of the number of times he'd seen people slow down past a road traffic incident, taking pictures on their mobile phones, and he often wondered how they'd feel if it was their mother, son or grandparent who was seriously injured. But then again they wouldn't even consider that, would they? He knew that most people never thought beyond their own skulls.

His thoughts were interrupted by Chloe jogging back up the driveway, her feet crunching on the gravel as she did so.

'Right, they're sending another unit down to help keep control,' she said. 'CID are on their way too. Shouldn't take them too long. If I keep a cordon around the scene, can you meet the SIO when he turns up?'

'Yeah, course,' Stu replied, beaming inside at the added responsibility he'd been given, albeit only a fairly small one. 'Who's the poor sod you've dragged out of bed at this time of the night, then?'

'Jack Culverhouse,' Chloe said, before leaning over to speak to the paramedic again.

Stu swallowed hard and looked back at Chloe. 'Uh, I don't suppose you want to swap, do you?'

4

The taller man might have had a height advantage, but he was nowhere near as well-built as the man who was standing in front of him, almost a full foot shorter. That didn't bother him, though. He had fury on his side.

'What do you mean "not quite according to plan"?' the taller man barked, his jaw clenched.

'There were... complications,' the smaller, stockier man replied, trying desperately to think of a way out of this situation. He knew he was in some deep shit.

'You only had one thing to do. What the hell went wrong?' The veins in front of his temples were pronounced, a sign of his vastly increased blood pressure.

The shorter man looked towards the floor, licking his lips and biting the bottom one. 'Her kids were there.'

'What? I thought you were going to wait until they were out of the way?'

'I was. I did. It was gone midnight, for Christ's sake. I didn't know the damn kid was going to get up, did I?'

The taller man ran a hand through his thinning hair, the other locked onto his hip. 'I told you we should have done this another time. During the day, when the kids are out. This is a fucking mess. One big fucking mess.'

'And I told you that would be a bad idea with witnesses about,' came the terse reply.

'Well this didn't exactly turn out to be a fucking brilliantly executed plan, did it?' the taller man shouted, spittle flying from his lips. Then, a little calmer, he added, 'Did the kid see you?'

The shorter man shook his head. 'She saw something, no doubt about that. There's no way she'd recognise me, though.'

'How can you be sure?' he asked. 'Do you even realise what this means? This could blow the whole fucking thing out of the water. We'd be fucked before we'd even started. Do you know what the hell's at stake here? Do you realise?'

'Yeah, I realise. Of course I fucking realise. But there's no way in hell she'd recognise me. No-one would. I made sure of that. I was dressed head to toe in black, for Christ's sake. I looked like a fucking ninja. What more did you want me to do?'

Letting out a noise that sounded a bit like a laugh, the taller man shook his head. 'Not gather an audience, perhaps? Might've been a good start.' He exhaled noisily, then lowered his voice. 'Did it work, though? Did you... y'know...'

The shorter man swallowed, hard. That wasn't a question he wanted to be asked. 'I don't know. She was making some weird gurgling sound. It could go either way.'

'Either way? Why the fuck didn't you just finish her off?' The taller man was growing more incredulous by the second. Pay peanuts, get monkeys, he thought. And he'd ended up with the runt of the litter.

'What, with her kid standing there watching? Do me a favour.'

'You were paid to do a job, Clyde. That means you fucking do the job, alright? That's how this works. You don't just stop and come home because there's a kid stood at the top of the stairs.'

'Yeah? So why didn't you do it then?' the smaller man replied, squaring up to him. 'If you think it's so easy, why didn't you go round there and do it? Or is it 'cause you didn't want to get your hands dirty? If you don't want to take responsibility for it, if you want someone else to do your dirty work, don't go complaining when situations change.'

The taller man laughed again, mainly out of disbelief. He certainly wasn't used to being spoken to like this. 'When situations change... Jesus Christ. You're telling me situations have changed? What do you suppose happens if Tanya Henderson lives? What then, Clyde?'

'I dunno. She was alive before, wasn't she?'

'Oh yeah, she was alive. She was definitely alive. And she was getting in the fucking way. You think someone like her's going to take this as a warning? If that was the case we'd have given her a warning. That's why we needed her gone.'

'Well what did you expect me to do?' the shorter man said, getting the distinct feeling that whatever he did would have been wrong.

'I expected you to do your job properly. And if you leave witnesses... Well, you don't leave witnesses.'

'What, so you're saying I should've killed the kid now? Jesus Christ, man.'

'I'm saying you don't leave witnesses,' the taller man said, his voice deadly serious. 'How you interpret that is entirely up to you.'

The shorter man put his palms out in mock surrender. 'Look, I'm sorry, alright? I don't know what else to say.'

'Say nothing,' the taller man replied. 'Nothing.' He sighed deeply, rubbing one hand across his stubbly chin as the other stayed planted on his hip. 'There's only one thing we can do.'

5

Wendy Knight had — somewhat miraculously for her — managed to get to sleep at a decent hour. It was a truism that a huge percentage of police officers — detectives in particular — had problems sleeping and Wendy was definitely one of those statistics. Then again, anyone who'd been through what she'd had to go through over the past couple of years would probably have trouble sleeping too.

It was never going to be a life of plain sailing working for Mildenheath CID, but Wendy had experienced her fair share of trauma recently. Not only had her first big serial murder case resulted in her suspecting that her love interest was somehow involved, but it had actually turned out that her own brother was the killer. Then, just as she'd been starting to come to terms with what had happened, she was given the crushing news that she had suffered a miscarriage. In case that hadn't been enough for Mother Nature in her testing phase, Wendy later had to deal with losing a fellow officer in a gunfight, as well as finding out — along with her team — that one of their own had been responsible for killing two sex offenders.

She slept peacefully, the emotional centres of her brain silently praying that they'd at least get some respite for the foreseeable future. Until the unreasonably cheerful marimba ringtone woke her up, that is. It was one of Jack Culverhouse's requirements that all officers in Mildenheath CID kept their phones on loud during the night. Wendy hated that particular rule, especially as she was such a light sleeper.

She blamed Frank Vine, a fellow Detective Sergeant. He was notorious for his ability to sleep through absolutely anything — ringing phones, his wife asking him to stop snoring, not to mention early morning briefings. It was probably something to do with the fact that Frank Vine's idea of keeping in shape was to resemble a circle. Wendy knew she couldn't talk, though — she'd been neglecting herself just as much over the past couple of years.

She fumbled for her mobile on the bedside unit, managing to find her book and the TV remote — and almost knocking over a glass of water — before she finally found herself staring into the glowing screen, swiping her finger across it to answer the call.

'Guv?' she said, having seen DCI Jack Culverhouse's name flash up on the screen.

'Wakey wakey, Snow White,' came the gruff voice on the other end of the line. 'We've got work to do.'

'What is it?' she asked, knowing it would be particu-

larly serious if she'd been called out at this time. Culverhouse only ever used his dark humour when there was a
major investigation going on. The rest of the time, he
seemed thoroughly bored with life.

'Can't say for sure at the moment,' Culverhouse
replied. 'Anything from attempted murder to not being
very good at walking through doorways.'

Wendy was far too tired to try and make sense of his
cryptic humour. 'What do you mean?'

Culverhouse sighed. 'Got a woman lying in her
doorway groaning like Chewbacca. The paramedics and
the first response kids reckon she's been attacked, but you
know what they're like. Don't know their arse from their
elbow.'

'The paramedics?' Wendy asked, just about starting to
wake up.

'No, the wooden tops. Wouldn't surprise me if we
turned up to find a cat stuck up a tree.'

Wendy rubbed the sleep out of her eyes. 'Right. Got an
address?'

'Yep.'

'Do you want to tell me what it is?' Wendy said, exasperated. She wasn't in a particularly good frame of mind to
deal with Culverhouse's terse replies.

'Get your arse out here and you'll find out, won't you?'
came the reply.

Wendy got up out of bed, adjusted her nightdress and
opened her curtains just a fraction, letting the glow from
the streetlight filter into her room. Parked up on the road

outside her house she could see Culverhouse sitting in his car, looking straight at her and waving. She saw him speaking into his phone a split second before she heard the voice in her ear.

'Nice tits. Now hurry up and get dressed. I haven't got much petrol left.'

Culverhouse drove as quickly and directly as he could to the crime scene, while Wendy sat in the passenger seat, looking out the window. She was glad there was very little traffic on the roads at that time of the night. As the car screeched around the corner into Manor Way, she could see the flashing blue lights up ahead and the sight of the poor victim's neighbours peering out from their front windows.

'That woman must have some kind of sixth sense,' Culverhouse said, pointing to the pathologist, Dr Janet Grey, as they pulled up outside the house. 'I swear she turns up before the crimes have even happened.'

Wendy didn't even get a chance to respond, as Culverhouse had his door open and his feet on the pavement within a second of the car coming to a halt.

'Dr Grey, my one true love,' he said as he strode up the front path and greeted the pathologist. 'You know, you're doing it completely the wrong way by constantly getting me out of bed.'

Janet Grey smiled with just one corner of her mouth. 'What can I say? It's been a long time.'

'Not as long as it's been for me, I can assure you. What have we got?'

'Not a whole lot at the moment,' Dr Grey replied. 'The paramedics have just taken her off to Mildenheath General. She was losing far too much blood to keep her in situ. Now we're just waiting on SOCO to come down and do their bit.' The Scenes of Crime Officers were the forensics team dedicated to investigating crime scenes.

'Right. Well I'd rather get our bit wrapped up before the place starts to look like a beekeepers' convention,' Culverhouse replied. 'Did you see the IP?'

Wendy, who'd just managed to catch up, raised an eyebrow at Culverhouse's use of the acronym for Injured Party. He usually stuck with 'victim' or, sometimes, something much worse. She wondered if perhaps he was softening in his old age and finally coming around to the world of modern policing. She doubted it, but she decided to file it away for future reference anyway.

'I did,' said Dr Grey in response to Culverhouse's question. 'And she didn't look good. Blunt trauma to the back of the head, as well as bruising to her upper back. Looks as though there was a significant blow to the left-hand side of her skull, too. I reckon that's the one that floored her first of all. Large heavy object, swung right-handed. With a fair bit of force, too, I'd say. I managed to get a few photos in case we need them, but the paramedics were keen to have her in for treatment. I told them that was fine. Hope you don't mind me doing your job for you.'

'No, not at all,' Culverhouse replied. 'In fact, you can grow a scrotum, put on a ten-year-old Marks & Spencer suit and go out and interview the family if you like.'

'I think I'll pass,' the pathologist said, smiling. 'There is a witness, by the way. The woman's four-year-old daughter. She's too upset to interview at the moment, but she went to a neighbour's and told them what had happened. The neighbour says the woman's called Tanya. He doesn't know her surname but says her husband is called John. We can have the house searched for ID once the front door area's been cleared by SOCO.'

'No other witnesses?'

'Not that we've found. Uniform have spoken to a few neighbours and the first they heard was when the first response car turned up. I'm not quite sure how you manage to bludgeon a woman half to death on her front doorstep without anyone seeing or hearing you, but there you go.'

'The mind boggles, Dr Grey,' Culverhouse said. 'So she's up at Mildenheath General now?'

'Yep. Specialist brain unit. Lucky she lives in Mildenheath, really. Otherwise she'd be on for a long helicopter ride.'

'You know, Dr Grey, you never cease to amaze me,' Culverhouse replied. 'That's the first time I've ever heard anyone say they're lucky to live in Mildenheath.'

Mildenheath General Hospital was a place Wendy had seen quite a lot of in the past couple of years. Aside from the usual work-related visits, it was where her brother, Michael, had been taken following a drugs overdose, where she'd been told she'd miscarried her baby and where her colleague Luke Baxter had died.

She wasn't keen on hospitals at the best of times, but the positive attitude of the staff at Mildenheath General always gave Wendy hope, though how they managed to remain cheerful despite the constant pressures they were put under, she had no idea. As was the case with most areas of the public sector, the government were continually provoking, intimidating and constricting what they were able to do, their budgets shrinking and workloads growing by the day. Regionally, quite a few hospitals had reduced their services or merged them into other hospitals. For some there had even been talk of closure, and Wendy was sure it wouldn't be long before that option was touted for Mildenheath.

Mildenheath's accident and emergency department was one of the busiest in the region, primarily due to its location near two major motorways and an airport, as well as being on the edge of the growing urban sprawl of Mildenheath itself. There were other hospitals within easy driving distance, but Mildenheath had the unfortunate advantage of being closest.

One of the hospital's most impressive facilities was that of the specialist brain injury unit, which was what Wendy was attempting to find as she wandered the corridors of the hospital, trying and failing to follow the confusing and contradictory signage.

Culverhouse had gone into the office to assemble the investigation team and get things moving on a practical level, leaving Wendy to speak with the doctors and try to ascertain what had happened based on the medical facts. Depending on what was uncovered in the early stages of the investigation, it could be necessary for a uniformed officer to be stationed on the ward for the protection of the patient, so the young male officer who'd first arrived at the scene, PC Stuart Easton, had accompanied her to the hospital. Based on what Wendy had seen in terms of the aftermath of the attack and the apparent ferocity of it, she felt pretty sure that the attacker had meant to kill Tanya, and her experience told her that anyone determined enough to try to bludgeon someone to death on their own front doorstep wouldn't let something like failure stop them from trying again.

For now, though, that would have to wait. PC Easton had been summoned by the A&E receptionist to deal with an unruly customer in the waiting area — something a number of Mildenheath's beat officers spent a large portion of their weeks dealing with.

Finally, after a lot of corridor wandering, Wendy found her way to the specialist brain injury unit on the fourth floor and introduced herself to the nurse on the ward desk. The nurse, who could only have been about twenty-four, took Wendy to one side to explain the situation.

'The doctor is with her at the moment, but it's looking pretty serious,' she said, trying to sound reassuring and professional. 'Any brain injury is serious, of course, but in this patient's case, the injury seems to have caused a bleed on the brain. That's all we know at this stage. Although it looks like the bleed is relatively minor, the senior consultant decided it would be best to put her into an induced coma. That's far less scary than it sounds, I assure you. Essentially it means we've sedated her heavily, which allows us to control her breathing and also allows us to protect her brain while it heals.'

'Is that normal at such an early stage?' Wendy asked.

'To be honest, no,' the nurse replied. 'Although the way she was attacked, with the trauma directed at her skull, means there are a lot of unknown variables. We don't know yet which areas of the brain have been damaged, or how badly. And that kind of trauma can be extremely distressing for a patient. Giving her brain the chance to heal with protection should help her.'

Wendy sighed. 'So we won't be able to talk to her then.'

'Well, no. She's in an induced coma. Or will be shortly,' the nurse said, looking up at the clock beside her. 'When she came in she was understandably quite distressed. She seemed very confused and was making some quite disturbing noises, so she wouldn't have been in any fit state to talk anyway. To be honest, for all we know she could already be permanently brain damaged. It's just too early to say at this stage.'

'You say she'll be in an induced coma shortly,' Wendy replied. 'So she isn't yet?'

'I'm not sure,' the nurse said. 'It depends if the drugs have been administered and how quickly they have their full effect. It's possible.'

'Can I see her?' Wendy asked.

'I'd have to speak to the senior consultant,' came the reply. 'I really don't see the need, though. She's certainly not able to talk, and she's not responding to auditory or visual stimuli. I really don't know what else to say at this stage.'

'I understand,' Wendy replied. 'But if I could just see her anyway? We do need to make sure that we've got all angles covered.'

'Sure. I'll just check with the consultant,' the nurse said, smiling.

As the nurse headed back onto the ward, Wendy was left for a few moments in the company of an assortment of posters, leaflets and notices plastered to the walls. Many of them looked like they'd been there for years — yet another sign of corners having to be cut in the National Health Service. Other than that, this part of the hospital seemed to be very technologically advanced. It had long been lauded as one of the leading neurosurgical units in the country, and Wendy could see why.

In all the time she'd been a police officer, she'd never been to this part of the hospital, but she could understand how people easily became fascinated with the inner workings of the human brain.

Just as she was beginning to contemplate exchanging one career in investigating diseased minds for another, the nurse returned.

'I've spoken to the consultant. He said it's fine to see her, but not for long. She's in a pretty fragile state at the moment.'

Wendy knew exactly how she felt.

8

It's both pitch black and blindingly bright at the same time. The bright lights are the first thing I remember. I remember seeing it before I felt the pain. But now I think about it, I'm not sure if I did feel pain. Just confusion. Not a lucid confusion, not trying to work out what was going on, but an almost peaceful acceptance that I could do nothing but submit to whatever was happening.

It's not that I don't remember anything of what happened; I remember actively knowing nothing. It's not a missing part of my memory: it's a period of complete darkness, as though someone covered my eyes and plugged my ears. I don't know how long that lasted, but I experienced it in real-time. That section, that passing of time, it isn't missing; it's there, but it's blank. Blank until I started to become increasingly aware of myself, though slowly at first.

I remember hearing sounds — bleeping, buzzing and whirring. At first I thought it was inside my own head.

Then I heard voices. I knew that I knew the words they were saying, but they still didn't make any sense. The link between hearing and comprehending didn't seem to be there. Still now, however long it's been, every noise is adding to the confusion.

I don't know if I can see or not. That sounds like an odd thing to say, but it's the only way I can think of describing it. My brain is compiling pictures, images, relating them to the sounds I'm hearing and the sensations I'm feeling. But none of them make any sense. It's almost like I'm watching an old black and white television set and constantly turning the dial — almost always an incomprehensible fuzzy static, but occasionally I get the fleeting glimpse of a badly adjusted picture. And then it's gone.

The worst thing is that I can't do anything. I have no control. I cannot move. The link between my brain and my body seems to have disappeared. I don't feel any pain — just confusion.

There's the sound of someone talking. A deep voice, like a man. It is the men that have deep voices, isn't it? Yes. I think it's that way round. The men who—

A blinding flash of red passes in front of my eyes, more bright and vivid than anything I've ever seen in my life. It jolts me, feels like an electric shock or a bolt from a stun gun.

I see cowboys. Cowboys from the old Wild West. As they charge towards me, staring into my soul, I see the spears they point towards me, their horses deep black, almost purple. Cowboys don't carry spears, I realise, and they instantly become knights in shining armour. I can hear the clanging of metal chainmail and the whinnying of the horses as they reach me. I feel a spear puncture my chest as the air rushes into me, the horses pushing forward, trampling me and forcing the air in and out of my lungs, regularly, rhythmically.

I hear one of the horses squealing a high-pitched shriek. Then again. And again. The noise fades and builds, each time morphing until it sounds like a person talking. A lighter voice, a higher voice. I recognise her words as questions, but still they make no sense. They're just words. They carry no meaning. And I feel like I'm choking, struggling to hold on.

I'm slipping.

Slipping.

Slipping.

9

'This is Mr Mills,' the young nurse said, introducing Wendy to the senior consultant. 'He's in charge of the patient's care.'

Wendy shook hands with the affable-looking man in front of her. Her first thought was that he would be quite attractive, if she was into older men.

'Call me Julian,' the consultant said, pulling back his hand. 'I don't suppose you have any information on who the woman is yet?' Wendy detected a slight Scottish lilt to the man's voice.

'We're working on that at the moment,' Wendy said as she watched the nurse leave the room, the early morning summer light starting to stream in through the window. 'She was attacked in her home, so it shouldn't take long to find out. What can you tell me about her condition?'

Julian Mills raised his eyebrows almost in mock defeat. 'Only what I've already told the nurses, I'm afraid. She was brought straight here by ambulance with a severe head trauma, and we did a CT scan straight away in order to try and ascertain what was going on. She was struggling for breath, but was still breathing on her own. She seemed to be conscious but unresponsive, which could be a cause for major concern. It could be the effects of shock, of course, but until we've done a more detailed analysis it's impossible to say for sure.'

'And she's in a coma now?' Wendy asked.

'Yes. What we'd refer to in layman's terms as an induced coma. In effect she's been heavily sedated to keep her body and brain activity relaxed in order to give her the best possible chance of recovery.'

Wendy nodded, looking down at the mass of bandages and wires on the bed in front of her. 'Can she hear us?'

'Perhaps. Some patients in comas do report being aware of what was going on, but not often so much in induced comas. The dose of barbiturates is pretty high.'

'What would you say her chances are?' Wendy whispered. 'Realistically.'

The consultant shook his head. 'Impossible to say. Even if we could calculate her chances right now, which we can't, it's liable to change drastically at any time. The first twenty-four hours are absolutely crucial. We can never predict how the brain's going to react to an injury.'

Wendy could see where he was coming from. How often did you read about people who tripped in the street, hit their head and died? Then, on the other hand, there were numerous stories about people being shot in the head at point blank range and surviving. She guessed some people just had an in-built survival mechanism.

'There's still so much about the brain we don't know,' Julian Mills said. 'I've been doing this job for over twenty years and I'm still learning things every day.'

'I know exactly what you mean,' Wendy said, thinking about her own job. It was a constant, never-ending learning curve. She was interrupted by the sound of her mobile phone ringing in her pocket. The screen showed Detective Sergeant Steve Wing's direct dial number. 'Sorry, just be a minute,' she said, raising her hand in apology and leaving the room to take the call. 'Steve?'

'We've got an ID on your woman,' Steve said on the other end of the phone. 'Tanya Henderson's her name. She's a journalist or writer of some sort. We've managed to contact her husband at work, and he's on his way to the hospital now. Reckoned it'll only take him about an hour and a half to two hours at this time of night.'

'Right, thanks Steve,' Wendy replied, trying to figure out where would be best to meet Tanya Henderson's husband. She knew it wouldn't be a great idea for him to see his wife in this state, particularly while she was still so unstable, but he might insist on it, as she'd done. 'What about the daughter?'

'She's with the neighbour, still. There's an officer with them. Get this — when they went back into the house, there was another one. A boy, eight years old. Tucked up fast asleep in bed without any idea what was going on.'

'Poor little thing,' Wendy said. 'Is he at the neighbour's too?'

'Yep. They're happy to keep an eye on them for now.'

'Right, good,' Wendy replied, before an instinctive flash of warning appeared in her mind. 'Steve, can we get someone over there? One of ours, I mean. Get the lowdown on the neighbours.'

'Lowdown?' Steve said, almost laughing. 'Don't think you'll need to bother. They're both about a hundred and twenty. I doubt either of them can lift their own pants up, never mind a baseball bat or whatever.'

'Still. Better safe than sorry,' Wendy replied. 'First people on the scene and all that.'

'If you say so. I'll give Frank a call. The guv said not to get him in until ten, but I could do with a laugh.'

Wendy tried to picture the look on DS Frank Vine's face when he got a call not only waking him up at the crack of dawn, but asking him to go and babysit a couple of pensioners. 'Good luck with that,' she said.

'Cheers. Any news from the doc?' Steve asked.

Wendy shook her head, even though she knew Steve couldn't see it. 'Nothing yet. They said anything can change in the first day or so. Right now it's a case of waiting and seeing how things pan out. They did a CT scan and there's a bleed on her brain, so they've put her in an induced coma.'

'Blimey, sounds serious.'

'Yeah. I'm sure she's felt better. Listen, let me know when you've found out a bit more about her, will you? In the meantime I'll try and find PC Easton. I could do with him here when the husband turns up.'

'Will do,' Steve replied. 'Debbie's due in any second and the guv's just updating the Chief Constable.'

Wendy allowed herself to smile. Detective Constable Debbie Weston was one of the most undervalued members of the team. She always worked quietly and without fuss, and she had a tendency to uncover information that no-one else could. Somehow Debbie had always been passed over for promotion to a higher position, but it never seemed to faze her. She just carried on regardless.

10

The Chief Constable's office was somewhere Jack Culverhouse almost always felt appreciated. More so than he did in most other parts of the building, anyway. It was an office he wouldn't have minded having for himself one day, but he very much doubted if that day would ever come.

Charles Hawes, the present Chief Constable, only occupied the office when he wanted to get away from the county's police headquarters at Milton House, which, to be fair, was most of the time. Almost all of the police resources in the county had been relocated there, as well as some regional services. It was all part of the current fashion of police mergers and 'service and efficiency sharing', which was government speak for 'we're cutting your funding'. Unfortunately for Mildenheath, the county's current Police and Crime Commissioner, Martin Cummings, was a particular fan of praising the virtues of 'streamlining' services whilst in the same breath bemoaning the government cuts that caused them.

As far as Jack Culverhouse was concerned, the politics could go to shite. All he was interested in was doing his job to the best of his ability and in the only way he knew how. When politics got in his way, he was the first person to speak out about it — and loudly, too — but for the most part he considered them all to be a big bag of bastards. For as long as Charles Hawes was the Chief Constable, though, Culverhouse knew his arse was covered. Hawes was of the same old school approach as Jack — two of the last people on the force who knew what real policing was about.

'So are we potentially looking at a murder case, then?' Hawes asked, the unspoken sentiment being that he was deeply concerned, as was everyone else, about the relatively high murder rate in Mildenheath. Although their success rate in catching killers was also extraordinarily high, this did little to assuage the fears of Martin Cummings, who was only ever interested in headline figures and statistics. Rising murder rates were not the sort of headline figures and statistics he was keen on.

'We don't know yet,' Culverhouse replied. 'At the moment, no, but early signs indicate we've probably got enough to charge with attempted murder. No early suspects, though. The husband was working away. He does something in financial services, apparently. Although that's coming from the geriatrics next door, so it could be anything.'

'He out of the frame, then?'

'Seems to be. We'll get triangulation on his phone to confirm that, but my spidey senses aren't exactly tingling.'

'No signs of forced entry? Nothing stolen?'

Culverhouse curled his bottom lip and raised his eyebrows. 'Impossible to say if anything's been stolen. The husband will be able to confirm that when he gets back. But no, no signs of forced entry. The four-year-old daughter reckons she got up because she heard the doorbell. We've not spoken to her properly yet, though. We'll need to get child protection officers in for that. Cover our arses.' Culverhouse, like many experienced officers, had seen cases thrown out of court because the prosecution had been unable to prove that a young child witness had been interviewed without any leading questions.

A defence team would, of course, try to latch on to anything that they thought would plant a seed of doubt in a judge or jury's minds, so an enormous amount of time was spent trying to ensure that the evidence was sound, with all potential loopholes tightened and any holes well and truly plugged. The Crown Prosecution Service, who reviewed the evidence and informed the police of whether or not a charge would stick, tended to err on the side of caution. Getting someone to court was an expensive and laborious process, and it wasn't a decision that was ever taken lightly.

'There's something else I wanted to tell you, Jack,' the Chief Constable said, taking a sip of tea from his mug. 'There's a new officer joining your team. Called Ryan Mackenzie. Young, keen, works hard. Specific roles are up to you, of course, but I think Mackenzie would be ideal to fill Luke Baxter's boots.'

The mention of Luke's name always brought back memories for Jack. He'd seen Baxter as his young protégé — someone who could be moulded to carry on his own legacy when the time came for him to retire noisily. One stray bullet had ended all that.

'Sir, I really don't think we need anyone else,' Culverhouse said. 'Not at this stage. At the moment this is an assault case. Possibly attempted murder at best. We're more than fine with the team as it is.'

'It's potentially a murder case, Jack,' Hawes said. 'We don't know if Tanya Henderson's going to make it through the day yet. If that's the case, the shit's going to hit the fan. She's a journalist on a national newspaper, for Christ's sake.'

'She's freelance,' Culverhouse replied.

'I couldn't give a shit if they pay her in bloody Pokemon cards. The point is the pressure's going to be on us to get a result.'

'Which is even more reason not to have to spend time introducing someone else to the team,' Culverhouse said, his tone of voice changing to one that Hawes was more than familiar with. 'We need to be able to move quickly. I don't think the Inquirer will be particularly chuffed if they find out I've spent the first couple of days teaching an office junior how to photocopy a witness statement.'

Charles Hawes stood up. 'Jack, Ryan Mackenzie is a

bloody good officer. Fantastic track record in a short space of time, lots of ambition, just the sort of person you need.'

Culverhouse knew exactly what sort of person he needed on his investigation team, and he also knew that person wasn't going to be working on it again.

'No ifs, no buts,' the Chief Constable continued. Ryan will join you later this morning. Understood?'

Culverhouse ground his teeth, feeling the muscles in his neck tense. 'Understood, sir.'

11

By the time John Henderson had got back to Mildenheath, Wendy had managed to swing a room next to the specialist ward his wife was on. It was neatly furnished but still had that look of a hospital trying and failing to make a room feel homely. There were two sofas, both of a coarse yellow fabric and not particularly comfortable, positioned at right angles to each other. A fern in a big brown plant pot was placed in one corner, and a kids' play area took up another corner. This was where families and relatives were given bad news, Wendy realised. And it was about to happen again.

PC Stuart Easton, whom she'd wanted to be with her when she met the husband, had been called away to deal with another incident in town, leaving her on her own.

As Wendy was busy writing up her notes into long-hand, ready for logging back at the station, John Henderson was brought into the room by a ward nurse.

'Where is she?' he asked, clearly distressed, and seemingly a little confused as to why he'd been ushered into this room rather than being taken straight to his wife.

'She's on the specialist ward. The doctors are looking after her. John, isn't it?' Wendy replied, holding out her hand and smiling at the man in front of her.

'Yeah,' came the soft response as Tanya Henderson's husband shook her proffered hand.

'Firstly, it's important to try and think clearly and calmly. I'll speak to the doctors about taking you through to see your wife, but first of all we need to try and ascertain what's happened, okay?'

John swallowed hard and nodded. 'Yeah, okay.'

'So you were working away, were you?' Wendy rested the nib of her biro on top of the notepad, jotting down everything he said.

'Yeah, I have to work away quite a bit. I work for the Financial Conduct Authority. I do spot checks on banks and lenders to make sure they're complying with FCA rules. All very boring, really.'

'No, it sounds really interesting,' Wendy lied. 'So you were away from the house between which dates?'

'I left the night before last and had three days in various places up north. I was due to come back the day after tomorrow. Are the kids alright?'

'They're fine,' Wendy said. 'They're with a neighbour.'

John Henderson nodded slowly.

'Do you know of anyone who might have wanted to harm your wife?' Wendy asked, as gently as she could.

John looked up at the ceiling and sighed. 'Yeah, plenty. We always said this would happen one day. I kept telling her, we needed to get CCTV put on the house or something, but she wouldn't have it. She said she didn't want them to think we were intimidated.'

'Them?'

'She's an investigative journalist. "Them" is just about everyone she's ever written about or looked into.'

Wendy didn't say anything, but in her mind she thought it unlikely that Tanya would've been attacked by someone she'd written about in the past. It would be too obvious. After all, where was the first place the police would look? Besides which, investigative journalists rarely went to press unless they had a pretty cast iron case to print. In that situation, what would be the point in having her attacked or killed afterwards? The damage would've already been done. All that would do is point another big finger at themselves. Wendy doubted whether anyone with enough of a brain to get involved in large scale corruption would simultaneously be stupid enough to resort to revenge. No, there had to be more to it than that.

'What about current investigations?' she asked. 'What has she been working on recently?'

'I have absolutely no idea,' John replied. 'She never says a word to me about her work. She never says anything to anyone. Not until it's all out in the open, anyway.'

'What about notes? She must have filed things away somewhere.'

'No, she does everything digitally. She uses code

names and pseudonyms for people and encrypts all of her data. Even if you got hold of her computer, you wouldn't be able to do anything with it.'

Wendy winced inwardly. The last thing she wanted was to have to deal with the tech boffins. She wondered if she might be able to call on Xavier Moreno up at Milton House to help her out. Even though it wasn't technically his job, Xav had used his expertise in administrating the force's computer network to help her out once or twice before, and if she was being completely honest, she had quite a large soft spot for him. 'Do you know what sort of encryption she uses?' she asked John Henderson.

'No idea. I'm not really up on all the technical stuff. Look, can you take me to my wife please? I want to see her.'

Wendy very much doubted whether John would really want to see Tanya in the state she was currently in, but she told him she'd see what she could do. A few minutes later they were standing at the side of Tanya's bed, looking down at her bruised body.

'She's in an induced coma,' Julian Mills, the senior consultant, told John. 'The idea is to slow her brain down, reduce the electrical activity and start to reduce the swelling. It's something we have full control over, and when we're confident that she's responding positively we'll be able to reduce the sedatives and slowly bring her round.'

'Can she hear us?' John asked.

'We don't know at this stage. Obviously she's not able to respond, but the early signs are that her brainwave activity has some way to go yet. That's quite normal after the sort of trauma she's endured. Now, we've also inserted a probe into her skull to monitor her intracranial pressure. She's at the upper end of what we'd usually be comfortable with, but it doesn't seem to be rising at the moment. We're keeping a watchful eye to make sure that continues, and hopefully the induced coma will bring it back down to normal levels.'

'Are there risks? John asked, unable to take his sad eyes away from his wife.

'There are risks with any medical procedure, but this is quite a common thing to do in this situation. The risks won't usually be connected with her brain, though. We're talking about things like chest infections.'

'Chest infections? How would a head injury cause a chest infection?' Wendy asked.

'The injury wouldn't,' Julian Mills replied. 'It's the induced coma. The high levels of barbiturates that bring about the comatose state also affect the cough reflex, so there's a possibility of matter building up in her lungs. She can't cough to clear it, see. There are some people who state that barbiturates lower the immune system, too, but I wouldn't be too worried about that unless the patient was already immunocompromised.'

'No. No, she's always been a very healthy person,' John said.

'Then I'm quite sure she stands the best chance possible. As I say, though, it's still very early days. Your wife is very ill.'

Wendy looked down at Tanya Henderson, lying there with tubes going to and from her mouth, controlling her breathing. There were wires connected to her skull, which was partially covered with a bandage and partially shaven, her long blonde hair reduced to mere stubble. And as she looked down she thought a thought she often had when faced with a particularly brutal and inexplicable crime: who in their right mind could ever want to do a thing like this?

12

There was no sweeter sound to soothe Jack Culverhouse's soul than the sound of a buzzing incident room. He'd just come to the end of his morning briefing — something he would rather have had DS Knight on board for, but she was at the hospital, speaking to John Henderson.

The idea of the morning briefing was to assemble his team and tell them what was known so far. At the moment, that was very little, as was usually the case at the first morning briefing. After all, it was the responsibility of the investigation team to get to the bottom of what had happened, and the first morning briefing generally resembled square one.

There was always a surge of adrenaline at this stage of the investigation, mainly fuelled by the realisation that there was a major, serious crime to investigate. It was the excitement of the unknown. It also meant that they wouldn't simply be going through the motions, following up on the usual fraud and white-collar cases, or, in Jack Culverhouse's case, doing all he could to finally try to link the local white-collar crimewave to Gary McCann, a man who was widely known as one of the dodgiest bastards in the area, but who was cagier than an aviary and more slippery than an eel.

The officer Jack tended to work closest with was Wendy Knight. They didn't always see eye to eye, to say the least, but he couldn't deny that they seemed to work well together. Secretly, he admired her for the way she worked: always within the rules, but still always getting results. Besides which, she was a hard bitch; she always bounced back and never let anything finish her off. He'd come far closer to admitting defeat in recent years than she ever would.

Also on the team were Frank Vine, a Detective Sergeant who never seemed far off retirement but who didn't seem to put enough energy into anything to ever need to retire; DS Steve Wing, a man in his forties who was happier munching his way through the office vending machine and drinking gallons of coffee than he was going out on the beat; and Debbie Weston, a Detective Constable who quietly but assiduously kept the team on track and often provided the breakthrough in investigations — not that Culverhouse would ever admit it. Today, though, the five were to become six again.

'I had a chat with the Chief Constable this morning,'

he said, addressing the team, 'and he told me we've got someone new joining us. Young lad by the name of Ryan Mackenzie, apparently.' He looked around the room. 'Although he's not exactly made the best first impression by not bloody being here.'

'Do we need someone else?' Steve Wing asked, his narrowed eyebrows making it clear that his answer to his own question was an emphatic no.

'Preaching to the choir, Steve,' Culverhouse replied. 'Not my choice. Quite what the idea is with taking bodies off the streets when they're already short staffed, I've no idea, but management need to earn their wages somehow. A shit decision's better than no decision, apparently.' He shook his head slightly before getting down to business. 'Right, Debbie, I want you looking into Tanya Henderson's work. Get online and look into the archives, see what you can find out about the articles she's written before. Frank, I need you to start looking at phone records and financials. See if there are any anomalies.'

Culverhouse was interrupted by the door to the incident room opening. A young, short, slender woman peered around the door. 'Ryan Mackenzie?' she said.

'What about him?'

The young woman raised an eyebrow at Culverhouse. 'He's here.'

'Right. Good. Send him in then,' Culverhouse replied, turning to head back to his desk. As he went he heard the sound of the door closing behind him, shortly followed by Frank and Steve chuckling to each other. When Culverhouse turned, he saw the young woman standing a few feet further forward from where she'd been a moment before. 'Sorry, am I missing something?' he asked.

'I've no idea. You asked me to send Ryan Mackenzie in. So I came in.'

Culverhouse blinked a few times. 'You're Ryan Mackenzie?'

Ryan looked herself up and down mockingly. 'Last time I checked.'

'You're a bird,' Culverhouse replied.

Ryan placed a hand over each of her breasts, as if noticing them for the first time. 'Bloody hell. So I am. Whaddya know? Although we do tend to prefer "woman".'

'You're the new officer?'

'Well I can see the tales of your legendary skills of detection were all true, Detective Chief Inspector. This my desk?' Ryan pointed to an empty workstation.

Culverhouse looked at Ryan, raised his eyebrows in defeat and walked over to Steve Wing.

'Steve, I want you to go door to door on Tanya Henderson's street. Speak to the neighbours, see what they heard and what they saw. Keep your eyes and ears peeled, and get the neighbours checked out, too. See if any have previous. And you can take *Ryan* with you, too,' he added, saying her name as if she'd just invented it thirty seconds earlier.

Ryan smiled at Steve and opened the door behind her, waiting for him to follow. Steve took one look at Culverhouse and decided to do as he was told.

There were a few moments of silence after Steve and Ryan left the room, until Frank Vine decided to try and break through the atmosphere.

'Looks like you've met your match there, guv.'

Culverhouse stared at the door. 'Not fucking likely.'

13

Steve Wing was particularly proud of his BMW 3 Series. It was a car he'd wanted for a long time, and even though he'd now had it for three years or so, it still felt like a brand new car to him. It also meant he didn't have to walk anywhere, which was nice.

The journey from Mildenheath Police Station to Tanya Henderson's house took a little longer than usual with the morning traffic, and it seemed even longer due to the fact that Ryan apparently wasn't the sort of person to make small talk unless she absolutely had to.

'So. You into cars?' Steve asked as he pulled on the handbrake at a set of traffic lights.

'Not really.'

Steve nodded. 'You drive?'

'I can, but I don't.'

'How do you get to work then?' he asked.

'Bike.'

Steve could see he was getting nowhere fast. 'You mean a motorbike? Or—'

'Pushbike. Zero carbon.'

He nodded again, trying to look interested. As far as he was concerned, carbon was something the scientists could deal with. His pleasure was in driving fast cars. 'So do you live local, then?'

'Not far,' Ryan replied. 'Ten minutes on the bike.'

'That's not bad. Probably take you twice that in a car. This your first job in CID then?'

The traffic lights turned green and Steve accelerated away.

'Yep. It's where I want to be. Put my skills to good use for once.'

Steve allowed himself a cheeky smile. 'So what are your skills exactly?'

'Focus. Determination. Spotting a bullshitter a mile off.'

'Nice,' Steve said, unsure what else to say. 'We could do with a good-looking woman around the place.'

Ryan raised an eyebrow. 'Is that what it takes to be a good detective, then? A pair of tits and a cutesy smile? And there's me thinking you had to be, like, good at detecting or something.'

Steve could feel himself getting a little flustered. 'Well, no, that's not what I meant,' he said, trying to backtrack. 'I mean we need some young blood. We're not sexist or anything. Well, I'm not. Far from it. Couldn't be further from the truth. I love women. Not like that, I don't mean. I mean, we've got a few women in the team now. Three in fact. Half of us are women.'

'Good. Way it should be,' Ryan said.

'Yeah. That's what I've always said. Make it all equal. I mean, we're the same, aren't we? Men and women, I mean.'

Ryan looked over at Steve with a look on her face that said 'in your dreams, mate'.

'So, are you into all this sort of equality and stuff?' Steve asked.

'If by "into equality and stuff" you mean do I think that people shouldn't be discriminated against based on how many testicles they have, then yes. And so does the law.'

'Well yeah, obviously,' Steve replied. 'I just mean that—'

Ryan decided to do Steve the courtesy of not letting him dig himself into a deeper hole. 'So, this case. What leads do we have at the moment?'

Steve breathed a silent sigh of relief. 'Not many, to be honest. Well, that and just about everyone in a position of power.'

'Narrows it down nicely. So what's this? Illuminati conspiracy?'

'I doubt it somehow. I imagine if we're talking about the people at the top they'd at least do it properly. Not send some lowlife who can't finish the job properly and who panics and runs off when he sees a child appear.'

'What, so you'd rather he'd just carried on and blud-

geoned the woman to death in front of her daughter, then?'
Ryan asked, sternly.

Steve could feel himself getting flustered again as he
stammered, 'Well, no. I didn't— That's not what I—'

'Relax,' Ryan said, smiling for the first time during the
journey. 'I'm kidding. I know what you mean.'

Steve parked the car on Manor Way, a little way down
from Tanya Henderson's house. The road had been
blocked off a few yards further on, the cordon of police
tape intending to stop passers-by from getting too close and
having a peek at what was happening.

Steve flashed his warrant card at the uniformed officer
on the boundary. 'She's with me,' he said, thumbing a
gesture at Ryan.

'Where do you want to start?' Ryan asked.

'Probably best to stick with the neighbours closest to
the Hendersons and then move outward. The ones nearest
will be most likely to have heard something,' he replied,
walking up the path of the house next door to John and
Tanya Henderson's place. 'An elderly couple lives here,
apparently. They've been looking after Tanya's kids.'

Steve pressed the doorbell, and within a couple of
seconds a man of about eighty opened the door. His
advancing years were fairly apparent, but he still seemed
fit and sprightly.

'DS Wing and DC Mackenzie from Mildenheath
Police,' Steve announced. 'Can we come in?'

'Yes, of course,' the man replied, beckoning them
through to his living room, an open plan lounge-diner.

Tanya's children were sitting in the lounge area, the man's wife sitting with them, trying to keep them occupied. As they entered the room, she looked up at Steve and Ryan, a regretful look on her face.

'You're Mr and Mrs... Aldridge, is that right?' Steve asked, glancing at his notepad.

'Yes. Larry and Margaret,' Mr Aldridge replied.

'And these must be Archie and Lola,' Steve said, walking over to the two children, who were sitting on a rug between two right-angled sofas, watching a kids' film on the TV.

'We really don't know what to say to them,' Margaret Aldridge said quietly as she rose to her feet to speak to Steve, her knees groaning and cracking as she did so. She lowered her voice even more. 'We just told them that Mummy had been hurt and that she needed to go to the doctor to have it made better. Do you think we did the right thing?'

'I don't know,' Steve said. 'I imagine so. I haven't got kids.'

'We never did either,' Larry Aldridge said. 'We're just trying to keep their minds occupied until their dad gets here. We don't want to do the wrong thing.'

'I'm sure you're doing absolutely fine,' Steve replied, 'but I'm afraid I do need to get your side of the story on record.' He nodded to Ryan, indicating that she should start taking notes.

'There's not really a whole lot to say,' Larry said, shrugging. 'We didn't see or hear any of it — just the aftermath. I was woken up by the sound of the letterbox flapping, which it sometimes does in the wind, but not like this. And it wasn't a windy night. Then I heard a knocking noise at the door, so I went down.'

'Fortunately, I was still fast asleep,' Margaret interjected, 'because there's no way I would have let him go down there otherwise. I dread to think what might have happened then.'

'I went down,' Larry continued, 'and I could see someone small through the frosted glass. I thought it might be kids playing silly buggers, but when I started to unlock the door, I could see that the kid was still there. I opened it on the chain at first, then recognised little Lola from next door. She said her mummy had been hurt and that we needed to help.'

'By this time I'd woken up,' Margaret added. 'I looked out of the top window and I could see the light coming from the doorway next door. I couldn't see Tanya at that point, but it was obvious the door was wide open.'

'Yeah,' Larry agreed. 'Well, I opened the door properly and stepped out to see what had happened. That's when I saw Tanya on the ground. I took Lola inside, handed her over to Margaret, and immediately called the police.'

'And then what happened?' Steve asked, after a moment's silence.

'Then Margaret asked Lola where Archie was. She said he was in bed. So I went next door and fetched him.'

'You went into the house?' Steve asked.

'I had to. I couldn't just leave him there; as soon as he

heard the noise and commotion he would've woken up, come down, and found his mum like that. We water their plants and keep an eye on the place for them when they're away, so I used my spare key and went in and out of the back door.'

'It's actually round the side, but they call it the back door,' Margaret added.

Steve paused for a moment. 'I might be getting this wrong, but did you not tell the first officers that you didn't even know Tanya's surname? Yet they've given you keys to their house?'

Larry blinked a few times. 'Well, yes. It was early. I couldn't really recall it. Besides, I don't know if they've ever mentioned it.'

'Do you not ever have to take parcels in for them? Anything like that?' Ryan asked.

'No, not really. Tanya, she often works from home, though I don't really remember them having many things delivered to the house. Maybe once or twice, and we've picked their post up for them when they've been away, but we've never looked too closely at the names on the envelopes. Why would we?'

'I thought it was Henshaw or Harrison or something like that,' Margaret said, 'but I've never really thought about it. To us, they were just Tanya and John.'

Steve nodded, trying to work out whether Larry and Margaret were just innocently naïve and forgetful, or whether there was something a little odder about them.

As he looked at Ryan, he realised she was wondering the same thing.

14

In the early stages of an investigation, it seemed as though some aspects flew by really quickly, whilst others almost immediately ground to a complete halt. Getting clearance to search a crime scene was particularly slow at times, and this case was no exception. Only once the Scenes of Crime Officers had finished combing the front doorstep area was it cleared for CID officers to enter and search the house.

It was a constant frustration to CID that they were often unable to enter a scene and look for evidence immediately, but unfortunately this procedure was a necessity. Not only was there the possibility that they could contaminate the scene or destroy minute pieces of evidence — fingerprints, specks of blood, single hairs — but when the case got to court, the defence lawyer could have it thrown out within seconds if there was any doubt as to the legitimacy of the evidence. It really wasn't a risk that was worth taking.

Tanya Henderson's house looked just like any other of its type. It was definitely a lived-in family home, but it had been kept clean, neat and tidy. The kids' toys had been put away, save for one or two that were left out in the living room, and the remote control sat jauntily on the arm of the leather sofa, where it had been resting since its last user had pressed the red 'off' button. In the kitchen, the dishes — now bone dry — sat on the draining board, ready to be put away, and that week's shopping list was attached to the fridge with a magnet bought on holiday in Morocco.

Wendy was certain that almost every house on this road would look much the same. Decent-sized middle-class family homes full of decent-sized middle-class families, the dad working in the city whilst the mum worked from home, waiting for the kids to finish school. It sounded stereotypical, but in this part of town it was often true. Wendy had seen it many times and considered it a soulless way to live.

Tanya's office gave away no clues to anyone who didn't know what its occupant did for a living; it could have been anyone's home study, save for the fact that it seemed to be far more heavily used. This wasn't just a computer room with a small filing cabinet full of mortgage statements and car insurance documents — it was obvious that someone worked in here regularly, but there was nothing to specify what that work was.

Wendy didn't expect to find anything that would explicitly tell her what Tanya had been working on recently. She knew already that Tanya's working practices were extremely secretive and that she went to great lengths to conceal her information and protect her sources. But still, there had to be something somewhere — some name or place jotted down on a piece of paper, a phone number perhaps, or an important document that hadn't yet been destroyed. Tanya's laptop computer had already been taken in for forensic examination, and Wendy was due to receive the report any time now. It would all be gobblede-gook to her, of course, but she had a plan for decoding it — the plan she'd been thinking of for a while.

There was an A4 leather-bound diary on Tanya's desk, and when Wendy opened it — noting that it seemed to be well thumbed — she was surprised to see that not a single page had anything written on it at all. That seemed bizarre. Either Tanya had been using this diary purely to see when certain dates were, or there was something far stranger going on. Who would have a well-used diary with abso-lutely nothing written in it?

Wendy stood in the middle of the room, looking around her. It was extremely frustrating — lots of books, lots of artefacts, but absolutely nothing that fitted together. It was almost as if the office and its contents had been designed to confuse, to throw people off the scent. Was that a deliberate ploy on Tanya's part? Wendy assumed so.

Just then, her phone pinged, the sound of an incoming email. She swiped the screen, typed in her four-digit pass-code, and quickly read the message. As expected, it didn't mean a whole lot to her, so she closed down the email app and opened up her contacts list. After scrolling down for a while — the names whizzing up the screen in front of her — she found the one she wanted. She tapped 'Call' and waited for the phone to connect.

'Xav?' she said, trying to sound as friendly and personable as possible. 'It's Wendy.'

'Oh, hi Wendy,' came the reply. Wendy could tell from his voice that he was pleased to hear from her, the thought making her smile.

'Listen, I need your help again. I've got a preliminary report from forensics on an IP's laptop. It makes absolutely no sense to me, as usual. I was wondering if you might be able to help me decode it?'

'Sure. Email it over and I'll take a look.'

'Actually, it's quite a delicate case. I was thinking it might be best to go through it in person. Perhaps if you wanted to come over to my place, I could cook us dinner and we could go through it.' Even though she'd been thinking of doing this for a while, Wendy was still surprised by her own forthrightness.

Xavier Moreno paused for a few moments. 'Okay, sure. Sounds good. When were you thinking?'

'How about tonight?' Wendy replied. 'Eight thirty? I'll text you the address.'

'Sounds like a plan. I'll see you tonight.'

The conversation over, Wendy allowed herself a couple of moments to smile. Up until recently, she wouldn't have felt comfortable doing this. She still wasn't sure she was entirely comfortable now, but she knew it was a start. She wouldn't ever be able to put the experience with Robert Ludford completely behind her, but this was a step in the right direction.

All that aside, though, Xavier was a smart guy. If anyone could help her decipher the digital clues that could lead to Tanya Henderson's attacker, it was him.

15

Although Culverhouse usually liked to station himself at a desk in the main incident room with the rest of his team, there were times when he didn't want to be amongst the hubbub and instead retreated into his own office. This was one of those times.

The situation with his wife had, of course, been playing on his mind for years. He'd gradually managed to deal with it and push it to the back as time had gone on, but since her return and subsequent re-disappearance, it had been eating away at him again. And this time it wasn't showing any signs of going away.

He picked up his mobile phone, scrolled through the contacts list, and tapped on the screen to call Antonio García. García was an Inspector with the Spanish police in Alicante, on the eastern coast of Spain. After Culverhouse had worked with him on a cross-border case a while back, the pair had struck up a friendship. The last time they'd spoken wasn't too long ago, when Culverhouse rang him to try and get some information on his wife's whereabouts. After all, the last he'd heard, she'd been living in Spain. It was García who'd told him he could find no record of Helen, and that he thought it very unlikely she'd been out there at all.

Culverhouse, however, wasn't giving up that easily. He didn't want odds or degrees of likeliness — he wanted cold, hard facts. It was something he needed in every area of his life.

'Jack, what a pleasant surprise,' came the greeting of Antonio García as he answered the call. 'I hope the weather is nice in Mildenheath.' The constant jibes about comparing Mildenheath's weather to that of Alicante were something García took enormous pride in.

'Yeah, lovely. I'm sitting here in my Speedos eating a Solero. I hope it's pissing it down over there.'

García laughed. 'Blue skies, my friend. Beautiful weather. So what can I do for you? You want a holiday?'

'Too bloody right I do,' Culverhouse replied, 'but not on the Costa del Crime. Talk about a bloody busman's holiday. No, I need another favour from you, Antonio.'

'Another one? I should start charging.'

'Yeah, sounds about right,' Culverhouse replied. 'Even the poxy taxi driver wanted a five-Euro tip for chucking my suitcase in the boot last time I was over. I was half expecting a surcharge for breathing in the front seat.'

García let out a big belly laugh. 'Still, where would you rather be?'

Culverhouse chose not to answer that question. 'When I called you last time, you said you couldn't find a record of a Helen Culverhouse living in Spain.'

'That's right,' García replied.

'And you said you didn't *think* she could have stayed in Spain for long.'

García was silent for a moment before he spoke. 'Yes.'

'What did you mean by that?' Culverhouse asked.

'What did I mean? I meant that I didn't think she could have stayed in Spain for long.'

'But it would be possible?'

Culverhouse could hear García sighing at the other end of the line. 'Anything is possible, Jack. You know how it is. People have ways and means. There was no record of a Helen Culverhouse on social security or any government records, but that just means she never saw a doctor, never earned a wage, never drove a car, never rented or bought a property, never opened a bank account... Do you see what I'm saying?'

'Yeah, I see exactly what you're saying,' Culverhouse replied, knowing full well that there was no way Helen could have lived off cash in a foreign country for eight-and-a-half years. He knew that Helen would have needed to renew her driving licence within two years of moving to Spain, and that she could only have renewed it with the Spanish authorities, which she clearly hadn't. And there was no way she would have had enough cash to buy a place or rent for that long. She hadn't touched their joint bank account before or after she left, and Jack very much doubted if she had any secret accounts of her own.

How she'd managed to do it was a complete mystery to him, but then again, Helen had always been an enigma. He'd never doubted the fact that she was alive and well — the note she left him had said that much, Somehow, Helen always had a plan up her sleeve and she always came up smelling of roses, no matter what. It was just her way.

'So, what are the options?' he asked García.

'How long is the piece of string?' the Spaniard replied.

Culverhouse was always tickled by García's usage of English idioms, but today he wasn't in the mood for laughing. 'What are you saying? She was living under a false name?'

'That's not so easy,' García replied. 'It's possible, but very difficult. It all depends on who she knew. If she didn't know any — let's say, shady — people in Spain, or any people who had links to Spain, it would be almost impossible for her to do that.'

Culverhouse was fairly sure Helen hadn't built up any links with Spain. They'd been there on a couple of holidays a few years back, but that was about it. No more so than anyone else. He felt guilty at not being able to be sure about this, though. The more he thought about it, the more he realised he'd known hardly anything about his wife. She'd just always been there, ready and waiting at home while he focused entirely on his work.

García continued. 'I didn't want to get your hopes up, Jack. And I still don't. It *is* possible she was here, but there's nothing we can prove. You need to keep all of your options open. Of course, you also have to think about the other alternatives.'

'Like what?' Culverhouse asked.

'Like did she ever come to Spain in the first place? Or was she trying to make you focus here, and not on the place she really went?'

'You mean, did she lie to me?' he asked, not liking where this was going.

García made a noncommittal noise. 'It's not for me to say.'

'No, but if you were in my shoes, what would you do?' Culverhouse said.

García was silent for a couple of moments.

'How well do you really know your wife, Jack?'

16

Shortly after lunch, Culverhouse reassembled the team for an update. By this point, most of them had completed the preliminary stages of their investigation.

'Knight. News from the husband?' he said, sitting on the edge of a desk and crossing his arms across his chest.

'Not a whole lot, to be honest,' Wendy replied, looking down at her notebook. 'Tanya never told him much about her work. She didn't tell anyone who didn't absolutely need to know, apparently. We've got her laptop and an external storage drive, which we believe has her files on it. Her husband, John, reckoned she used some pretty hefty encryption on it, though. I've passed it on to my tech contact at Milton House and he's having a look at it.' She somehow managed to say this last sentence with a completely straight face.

'What are the chances of us finding something?' Culverhouse asked.

'To be honest, guv, slim. If she used a level of encryption that'd stop the sorts of people she was investigating from getting their hands on it, I'm not massively confident that we'll be able to crack it.'

'That's what I don't get,' Ryan Mackenzie interjected. 'Why didn't the attacker nick the laptop and storage drive as well? If their aim was to stop her investigation, why would they leave all the data there?'

'Probably because they were spooked by the daughter,' Wendy said. 'I imagine their intention was to kill if not seriously harm Tanya, then take the laptop and storage drive. It just didn't play out that way.'

'In which case we're not looking at serious players, are we?' Ryan continued. 'If we were, they would've finished the job properly, surely?'

Steve Wing looked askance at Ryan. He was pretty sure he'd heard these words somewhere before.

'That's not a bad point,' Wendy said. 'Either that or it was nothing to do with any of her investigations.'

'So what other reason would someone have to try to bludgeon a young mother to death?' Culverhouse asked.

'Some sort of affair?' Frank Vine piped up. 'Might be the wife of someone she'd been sleeping with. Happens all the time.'

Culverhouse shook his head. 'I dunno. That doesn't seem right to me. Women tend to react differently when it comes to revenge. Out and out violence against the person isn't what I'd expect.'

Ryan raised an eyebrow, though she didn't say anything.

'Might explain why the attacker legged it when they saw the daughter, though,' Frank replied. 'Mother's instinct and all that. Maybe she suddenly realised what she'd done.'

'Still doesn't quite sit right,' Culverhouse said, after thinking about it for a moment. 'We'll see what we dig up when the techies have gone through her phone, but I wouldn't expect much on that front either.'

'I wouldn't be surprised if it was connected with her work in some way, though, sir,' Ryan said, picking up a selection of printed papers. 'I mean, she's done some pretty decent hatchet jobs in her time. She's single-handedly ended some pretty prominent careers, by the looks of it. She's investigated government corruption, misappropriation of charity funds, public finance scandals... All sorts of things. What's to say someone didn't get wind that they were being looked into and decided to put a stop to it? If they acted on their own, or if they weren't big players, it fits the cocked-up MO.'

'Doesn't really help us get any closer, though, does it?' Culverhouse said. 'Until we know *what* she was investigating it doesn't tell us anything.'

'No, but we might have a bit of a lead on that,' Ryan replied. 'Looking through the articles I found on the web, most of them were either published by or originated with the Inquirer. Tanya Henderson worked freelance, but she seemed to have pretty strong links to that paper and it looks like she gave all her big scoops to them first. Might be worth a trip down to their offices to see what they know.'

'Agreed. I'll give them a call and we'll pop down later this afternoon.'

Ryan shifted her weight onto her other foot. 'Ah. I can't do this afternoon. I've got a doctor's appointment at five.'

Culverhouse shook his head slightly. 'And?'

'And I was going to ask you if I could get off a bit early to get there.'

'Fine with me,' Culverhouse replied.

'But I was just thinking about going to speak to the people at the Inquirer.'

'What about it?' Culverhouse said, coldly. 'I never said you were bloody coming. I'll take Knight.'

Wendy looked up at him. 'Guv, I've got a long list of things here that I need to—'

'Sorry, Knight, I don't remember asking your permission.'

Wendy nodded, knowing from experience that it was best to leave Culverhouse to it when he was in this sort of mood.

'Steve, what did you get from the door-to-door stuff?' Culverhouse asked, overlooking Ryan Mackenzie once again.

'No-one saw or heard anything, guv. The first person to know of anything was the next-door neighbour, Larry Aldridge. The first thing any of the other neighbours saw or heard was the police and ambulance turning up. One house over the road has CCTV on the front of the building, but unfortunately they're too law abiding for their own good and it doesn't record anything past the end of their own driveway.'

'Brilliant,' Culverhouse said. 'Just brilliant. Why is it that everyone in this town seems to know everyone else's business until it comes to finding witnesses, and then Mildenheath turns into the Bermuda fucking Triangle?'

He stared at his team, but no one answered.

17

Debbie Weston was not only a fine Detective Constable, but she was also a trained Family Liaison Officer. She didn't tend to do much FLO work nowadays, but she was still called on fairly often to speak to witnesses or other people where a certain level of sensitivity was required. When Jack Culverhouse was around, that was more often than not.

Although Steve Wing and Ryan Mackenzie had already been to Larry and Margaret Aldridge's house, they'd only spoken fairly briefly to them and not at all to Tanya Henderson's young children. That, for her sins, would be Debbie Weston's job.

'What have they been told so far?' she asked Margaret Aldridge as she watched the woman's husband making three cups of strong tea. Their father was still at the hospital, keeping a bedside vigil, and hadn't yet seen his kids.

Margaret shook her head. 'Not much. What can we

tell them? Only that their mummy isn't well and she's being looked after by the doctors, and that we need to look after them until Mummy's better.'

Debbie smiled. 'That's good. We tend to find it's best not to give anyone false hope, but to keep things positive at the same time. It's a tricky balance.'

'Oh, I know,' Margaret replied. 'It's been horrendous, not knowing what to say to the poor things. I mean, you just don't, do you? It's not something you ever plan for.'

'No. And thankfully it's not something that happens to most people, but I have to say you're doing an admirable job.' Debbie smiled at her, hoping to relieve at least some of the tension in the room.

'Is there any more news from the hospital?' Larry asked, handing Debbie her cup of tea.

'Nothing yet. They reckon she's stabilised, though, which is a good sign. She's not getting any worse, at least.'

'But she's not getting any better?' Larry asked, frowning.

Debbie paused for a moment. 'Well, we don't know. There are lots of different markers for improvement, I understand, but I do know that the doctors are keeping a very close eye on her. That's the whole reason behind the induced coma.'

'I just can't stop thinking about it,' Margaret said. 'Those poor little blighters. Who on earth would do such a thing?'

'That's what me and my colleagues are trying to find

out,' Debbie said. 'Is it alright if I speak to Archie and Lola now?'

'Yes, of course.' Margaret ushered Debbie through to the living room, putting on a rather unconvincing smile as she said, 'Archie, Lola, this is Debbie. She's one of the people who are helping your mummy. But she needs to ask you a few questions so that you can help her too, okay?'

The children nodded, smiling slightly. It always struck Debbie how the innocence of childhood seemed to work in situations like this.

'Lola, do you want to go and help Mrs Aldridge in the kitchen for a couple of minutes? I'll talk to Archie first, and then I'll talk to you.'

Margaret took Lola through to the kitchen. She seemed happy enough to go.

'What are you watching, Archie?' Debbie asked, pointing to the television.

'Spongebob Squarepants.'

'Are you enjoying it?'

'S'alright.'

Debbie gave it a moment before speaking again. 'Archie, do you remember last night? Do you remember going to bed at home and then coming over here?'

Archie nodded.

'What do you remember?' Debbie asked.

'Don't know,' came the shy reply.

'Can you tell me about when you went to bed?'

Archie nodded.

'Who put you to bed?'

'Mummy.'

'And did you go to sleep?'

He nodded again.

'Okay. And do you remember waking up?'

Archie seemed to think about that for a moment. Then he nodded.

'Where were you when you woke up?'

'In my bed.'

'Okay, great. And who was there?'

Archie looked up at Larry, who was sitting in the armchair with his cup of tea. 'Mr Aldridge.'

Larry looked at Debbie and swallowed.

'And then what happened, Archie?' she asked.

'He said I had to go next door with him because something had happened.'

'Did he say what had happened?'

Archie shook his head. 'He said he would tell me later, but we couldn't stay in the house.'

'Then what happened?' Debbie could see Archie's eyes narrowing. 'It's okay,' she added quickly. 'You aren't in any trouble. We just need to find out what happened so we can help your mummy.'

Archie swallowed, then appeared to grow in confidence. 'Mummy always says not to go with strangers, but Mr Aldridge lives next door so I think he's okay. And I could tell that it was serious.'

'That's very sensible of you, Archie. Your mummy's right, but you did the right thing. What happened next?'

'We went downstairs and out the side door to Mr Aldridge's house.'

'Okay. Did you wake up at all before Mr Aldridge came in?'

Archie shook his head.

'Did you hear any noises?'

There was a pause. Then he shook his head again.

Debbie thanked Archie, then got him to swap places with his younger sister. She smiled as she saw Archie walking back into the living room with Lola, holding her hand.

When Archie was gone, Debbie started asking Lola some similar questions. Again, Lola said that her mum had put her to bed earlier that night and that she'd fallen asleep soon after.

'Do you remember waking up?' Debbie asked her.

'Yes,' Lola said, quietly.

'Can you tell me about it?'

Lola nodded.

'It's okay. Go on.' Debbie smiled encouragingly.

Lola blinked a few times before speaking. 'I heard the doorbell. I thought it might be Daddy.'

'I see. So what did you do?'

'I got out of bed and went to the stairs to look.'

Debbie steeled herself. 'Okay. And what did you see?'

'Mummy was lying on the floor,' Lola said, matter-of-factly.

'And did you see anything else?'

She nodded. 'A person standing near her.'

'Can you tell me what the person looked like?' Debbie asked.

Lola shook her head. 'He was wearing black. On his head and his legs and his... on everywhere,' she said, gesturing towards her torso.

'Okay. Did you see him doing anything?'

Lola shook her head again. 'Just standing. And then he ran off.'

'Did you see which way he ran?'

Again, a shake of the head.

'Then what happened?'

Lola started blinking again, quite rapidly. 'I went downstairs and I could see Mummy was hurt, so I went next door.'

'That's very sensible,' Debbie said. 'What did you do when you got there?'

'I knocked on the door and then Mr Aldridge came down and Mrs Aldridge took me inside.'

'Did you go back to your house at all?' Debbie asked.

Again, Lola shook her head.

'Thank you, Lola, you've been very helpful.' Debbie smiled; she never ceased to be amazed at the bravery and innocence of children.

If only all adults were the same, she thought.

18

Although Wendy was happy to have been asked to accompany Culverhouse to the offices of The Inquirer, she did have more pressing matters to attend to. Besides which, she asked herself, did it really need two officers to travel down to London? The team was short-staffed as it was, and while the addition of Ryan Mackenzie might help in the long-run, the time it would take for her to get up to speed with how things worked at Mildenheath CID would effectively make them even more short-staffed in the short-term.

As far as Wendy was concerned, this would be the perfect task to give to Ryan, having her accompany Culverhouse instead. She could shadow him and watch how things were done, even if they weren't usually the best ways of doing things. But Culverhouse was a stubborn old bugger. If he'd decided he didn't like Mackenzie, that was it. He'd do all he could to undermine her and show her who was really in charge.

While Wendy wouldn't have traded places with her in a million years, she quite liked Ryan. She reminded her a lot of herself when she first started out: keen to make a strong impression, and aware that she needed to stand up for herself in this male-dominated environment. But she'd since learnt that there were certain ways to do that — ways that worked and didn't get people's backs up. She was sure Ryan would pick that up soon enough — after all, she seemed like a smart girl — but then again, Culverhouse had been knocking around a lot longer, and he still had no idea how to work through a day without getting people's backs up.

The offices of The Inquirer weren't half as plush as Wendy had expected. She half thought she might end up walking through a big revolving glass door on Fleet Street, men in suits barging past her on their mobile phones as stories flew in across the news desk, while pictures of the paper's previous front pages stared down at her from every inch of available wall space. What she actually found was a rather mundane and run-of-the-mill office which might just as well have been that of a telemarketing firm.

Young school leavers sat around either in baggy Aran sweaters or thin t-shirts with the sleeves rolled right up, exposing their tattooed arms. She thought that if she closed her eyes and concentrated, it would probably smell of vinyl records and political pessimism.

They sat down in the waiting area, which was actually just a corner of the office that had three contraptions they called sofas but were actually just slightly padded platforms with no backs.

One of the journalists — a rolled-up-t-shirt one — came over to see if they wanted a drink while they were waiting. 'Coffee? Tea?' he asked, without saying hello or introducing himself.

Wendy said she'd have tea, Culverhouse opted for coffee.

'Americano? Cappuccino? Latte? Macchiato? Espresso?' came the next question.

'No, coffee,' Culverhouse replied.

'What sort of coffee?' the journalist asked.

Culverhouse just looked at him. 'In a mug.'

The journalist raised his eyebrows and walked off in the direction of the kitchen.

'Shouldn't have any trouble finding a mug,' Culverhouse said as the journalist left. 'There's a fucking dozen of them sitting out there in stupid jumpers.' Wendy wanted to laugh, but decided it would be best not to humour him. 'Says a lot about our national press these days. What's the betting that they're just sitting there churning out that "seven ways to tell your partner is cheating on you" bollocks for Twitter?'

'I think The Inquirer is a little more professional than that,' Wendy replied. 'They do serious investigative journalism.'

'Christ. That's even worse. Just think what the fucking redtop rags must be like.'

A few moments later the journalist returned with their

drinks, and Culverhouse took his minute cup of coffee without saying a word.

Before long, they were met by a woman in her mid to late fifties, who introduced herself as Susan Kellerman. 'I'm the editor,' she said. 'Do you want to come through to my office?'

When the three of them got to Susan Kellerman's office, she sat them down and perched on the corner of her desk, one leg crossed over the other, her hands planted firmly on one knee.

'So, how can I help?'

Culverhouse was about to tell her she could start by sitting down on a chair like a normal person, but Wendy saw that coming and got in first.

'As I mentioned on the phone, we wanted to talk to you a bit more about Tanya Henderson,' Wendy said. 'To get an idea about her working practises and to see if something she was investigating might be pertinent to our inquiries into her attack.'

'Her attempted murder, you mean,' Susan replied.

'Well, yes. Do you know what she'd been investigating recently?'

Susan Kellerman looked at them both for a couple of moments before speaking. 'You do know the Inquirer specialises in investigative journalism, don't you?'

'We had worked that much out, yes,' Culverhouse said. 'We're detectives, after all.'

'Then you'll be aware that we have to be extraordinarily careful when talking about our ongoing investigations. A lot of the work we do consists of uncovering corruption within the Establishment. That includes the police.'

'Are you saying that Tanya Henderson was investigating police corruption?' Wendy asked.

'I couldn't possibly say. Anyway, we have a policy of complete non-discussion of investigations in progress unless it is absolutely necessary.'

'One of your employees has been attacked, Mrs Kellerman,' Wendy said. 'And this is a police investigation. I really think it would be in your best interests to cooperate.'

Susan Kellerman crossed her arms. 'Firstly, Tanya Henderson is not an employee. She's freelance. Secondly, I can't tell you anything because I don't know anything. That policy of non-discussion extends to me, too. She told me nothing. And thirdly,' she added, crossing her arms, 'it's Ms.'

Wendy jumped in again before Culverhouse could put his foot in it. 'So you're saying you know nothing about what Tanya Henderson was investigating recently?'

'That's what I just said,' Susan Kellerman replied, without a hint of emotion in her voice. 'I'm afraid I've got just as much of an idea as you have as to why someone would want to attack her.'

With that, she stood up, gesturing at the door. 'Thank you for coming. You can see yourselves out, can't you?'

19

I'm suddenly aware of my consciousness, but not of time. I don't know whether I've been continually here, my mind whirring, or whether there's been a big gap. It's impossible to tell. I only know that I've thought stuff before, and that I've thought it here, but not when. There's no sense of time passing. I'm not even sure if it is. What if I'm dead? What if this is the afterlife?

No. There's no reason why I should be dead. Is there? I try to think. Think back. But memory doesn't seem to be a thing. It's all images, flashing lights and signs. Nothing concrete. Nothing that I can...

Again, I become aware. Aware that I am. That's the only way I can put it into words. I know it's not the first time I've been aware, but I don't know how many times came before, either.

A flash of orange.

A face. It's black.

A screeching sound.

I'm aware. I'm almost... I feel like I'm me. I know that sounds strange. It feels strange. The fact is that I don't know when the last time I felt like me was. It might have been years. It might have been seconds. This might happen all the time, over and over again, on repeat, like—

Like that film. Films. I remember films. The images. The noises. The one where the same day happened time and time again. Is that what this is? It's the outside world. Films are from the outside world. I need to hang on to that, need to...

Yes. There's something. I can only describe it as an abstract sense of knowing. The only problem is I don't know what I know. I'm trying to link it all up, trying to connect the...

Back to films. Yes. I know what films are. It's a concept. A strong concept. If I focus on that I can use it to anchor myself in reality. Try to go from there, remember, work out what's...

I remember some badness. I remember evil. I remember writing. Asking. Knowing.

I was working. There was a sound. I started to move. I saw something. I heard something. I felt something.

It all feels just out of reach... I'm trying to grasp it but I can't...

Dark.

20

Wendy got home from the offices of The Inquirer with a little over an hour to spare. That would barely be enough time to get ready, let alone start to get anything cooking. She hoped this didn't mean the entire evening would be a complete disaster. She showered, chose an outfit, and was just pulling a bottle of wine from the wine rack when the doorbell rang.

When she opened the door, she was pleasantly surprised to see that Xavier looked even better in his casual clothes than he did in his work suit. And in her opinion he usually looked pretty good in his work suit.

She ushered him through to her sitting room, which she'd had some trouble with earlier. She hadn't wanted to go the whole hog with candles, incense, and soft jazz music, but she had wanted to at least put the thought in Xav's mind that she might be interested. In the end, she'd opted for a bit of mood lighting and left it at that.

They were barely halfway through the first glass of wine and the usual pleasantries when Xav brought up the matter of Tanya Henderson's laptop.

'It's another one of those reports that has a lot of words but doesn't actually say much,' he said, smiling. 'I think these guys like to make themselves sound important by bamboozling people and making you go to them with any questions. Sad, really. That's why I want to get into that line of work. Shake things up a bit.'

Wendy smiled. She liked his ambition.

'Basically,' he continued, 'it's an access problem. Seems Tanya Henderson was pretty smart when it came to computer security. Either that or she had some help. When the laptop starts up it needs a username and password to get in. Nothing too strange there, but we can usually get round that. There's a setting that's enabled by default which allows you to boot the machine up from an external disk, or to boot it into a certain restricted mode. That's been disabled, though.'

'What, so you can't get in?'

'Nope. Not easily. Perhaps not at all. But there are two things they found out. Firstly, when they tried to examine the hard drive separately, they found that it was heavily encrypted. Not just by the operating system, but by another piece of software. They can't say for sure without looking into it further, but it looks like it might be something like TrueCrypt.'

'Is that good?' Wendy asked.

'It is for security. Not so much for us. This is just an educated guess based on what we know so far, but I'd be willing to bet that she's not using the simplest form of encryption on this bad boy. She'll have gone the whole hog.'

'Great,' Wendy sighed.

'That's not necessarily the end of the line, though,' he added. 'I must admit I went a little further and took it upon myself to call Tanya's Internet Service Provider.'

'Xav!' she exclaimed. 'You could get yourself into some serious trouble doing that. I shouldn't have even shown you the report, let alone got you involved in the investigation.' Even as Wendy spoke, she knew she didn't mean it. She was actually pretty impressed by the lengths he'd gone to and the potential risks he'd taken to help her.

'I know, but it needed doing. Anyway, I've got a friend there. Officially, no-one from the police has spoken to anyone at the company. It'll be fine. Point is, I got him to check the traffic routes from her network. They have logs of where data has gone in and out from. With that, we can potentially trace it.'

'And?' Wendy asked, hopefully.

'And every single packet of data that left or entered Tanya Henderson's machine went through a VPN: a Virtual Private Network. Basically, let's say I have a website and you want to go on it. You type in the address and your computer makes a connection to the website, which is just another computer, via your internet service provider. If you use a VPN, the connection goes from your computer and through a number of re-routing networks before it reaches the website. There might be a hundred different connections on the way, but it all happens in under a second. What that does is put a whole load of encryption and confusion in between the starting point and the destination.' He paused for a moment, thinking how best to describe it. 'Imagine a huge game of Chinese Whispers. Your computer never speaks directly to my website. The message is just passed on down the line, encrypted, decrypted and re-encrypted the whole way.'

'What, so the traffic to and from Tanya's machine is essentially untraceable?'

'That's about the long and short of it, yes.'

'Is there anything we can do at all?' she asked, though she wasn't feeling very hopeful now.

'It's tricky. There's nothing straightforward. The nature of computer security means it goes beyond what humans can do. We're talking billions of mathematical calculations every second, all based on random numbers. And to be honest, I'm not sure they'd even bother trying; if Tanya Henderson dies, it might be different, but they're unlikely to do much for an attack.'

'It's being treated as attempted murder,' Wendy replied. 'That should put it on a par with actual murder in terms of investigation power.'

'True, but they'll need to prioritise.'

Wendy sighed and drank more of her wine. 'There must be more we can do.'

'Unfortunately not,' Xav replied, raising his eyebrows. 'You see it in the news all the time. Even the FBI aren't able to unlock people's iPhones if they don't have the four-digit passcode. There's no way in hell Mildenheath CID are going to be able to crack some of the strongest encryption known to man.' He shrugged, smiling, before adding, 'Listen, I might have one idea.'

'What's that?'

'You're pretty highly regarded at Milton House. And you know how much I want to get involved with the major crimes unit in IT forensics. I was just wondering... Well, perhaps you might be able to request my involvement and suggest that my skills might be able to... You know. Then I could have a proper look at the machine, might be able to find something they haven't.'

'Do you think that'd work?'

Xav shrugged. 'You never know. But I can't promise anything, of course. Certainly not at the moment.'

'Well, in that case, we'd better move on to something else, hadn't we?' Wendy said, holding the wine bottle aloft.

Within an hour they were on their second bottle, and the conversation had moved on through a number of topics. They'd started talking — inevitably — about work, had spent a few minutes discussing Jack Culverhouse's recent eyebrow-raising comments and actions, going on through politics and society, and had just finished a two-person diatribe on the abysmal state of British TV. Wendy was happy, though. The conversation was flowing because the wine was flowing, and she felt more relaxed than she had done in a long time.

'Looks like you're going to have to leave your car here,' she said to him, gesturing at the empty wine glass sitting next to him on the coffee table.

'Ah. See, I thought ahead. I got a cab.'

Wendy didn't know whether to be impressed or worried by his presumptuousness. 'Blimey. That must've cost a bit. I always said we were paying civilian staff far too much,' she said, winking at him.

'Yeah, well, arrest me,' Xav joked back.

'Cab back'll cost even more. Especially this time of night. It's a fair journey, Xav.'

'It'll give me a chance to sober up, then, won't it?' he replied.

'Well, if you want to save the money and hassle you're more than welcome to stay here.' She smiled, before quickly adding, 'I mean, I've got a spare room.'

Xavier smiled. 'Don't worry. I presumed that was what you meant anyway.'

Wendy paused for a moment. 'As long as your wife or girlfriend doesn't mind, that is.'

Xavier laughed. 'I don't have a wife or girlfriend. I've told you this before.'

Wendy brought the wine glass to her lips, murmuring into the glass before taking a sip. 'Just checking.'

. . .

Two hours later, Wendy pulled her numb arm from under the dead weight of Xavier, who rolled over onto his side, taking the soft cotton sheets with him. She sat up and took a sip of water, looking over at him as he began to snore.

She smiled.

21

The morning briefing was far more subdued and far less eventful than it should have been.

There came a stage in every investigation where it felt like things were hitting a brick wall. That usually came after a few days or weeks, once the witnesses had been interviewed, the family spoken to and the evidence examined. In this case, however, things were a little different. There were no witnesses, no-one knew anything about what or who Tanya Henderson had been investigating, and there was seemingly no evidence to examine.

As things stood, their best hope was that Tanya Henderson would make a full recovery as quickly as possible and be able to provide them with all of the missing links. At the moment, however, that seemed like a bit of a long shot.

By lunchtime, the mood in the room had dipped enormously. A search through Tanya's bank statements and credit card bills had uncovered nothing out of the ordinary. Calls to her past work colleagues and associates had proved unfruitful. They were quickly running out of options.

Culverhouse knew that before long there'd be pressure from above to get results, though, mercifully, Tanya Henderson's family were being very understanding at the lack of progress the investigation had made thus far. Of course, if Tanya's situation were to take a turn for the worse, however, things would change. It would then become a murder case, which raised the stakes to a whole other level. The lack of evidence would prove to be a huge problem, particularly as they wouldn't then have the potential hope of Tanya being able to provide them with some of the information herself. Not only would the seriousness of the situation ramp up dramatically, but the one hope that would give them a chance of succeeding would disappear. That wasn't a possibility any of them wanted to entertain.

Sensing the mood in the room, Ryan spoke up. 'Why don't we all take a step back for a bit?' she said. 'Besides which, we could all do with some food. There's a new place in town I quite like which opens at lunchtime. How about I treat us all to lunch?'

Steve Wing was, unsurprisingly, the first person to latch on to the mention of food. 'Sounds good to me,' he said. 'I'm wasting away here.'

Culverhouse raised his eyebrows. 'The only thing that's going to make you waste away is a massive dose of leprosy, you fat fuck.'

'So, who's coming?' Ryan said, ignoring Culverhouse's remark, and keen to keep the mood from dropping even further.

'And who's going to man the phones?' Frank Vine said.

'Front desk, same as always,' Ryan replied. 'If anything interesting comes in, they can patch through to our mobiles. Anyway, we won't be long.'

'How far is it?' Frank asked.

'Not far. Fifteen minute walk, maybe?'

'Bugger that. I'll stay here and have my sandwich.'

'Suit yourself. You'll come, won't you guv?' she asked Culverhouse.

He seemed to squirm inwardly, before looking over at Frank, who was unwrapping a very unappetising sandwich.

'I was just going to stay here with Frank, but on second thoughts...'

In the end, the walk took them closer to twenty minutes, with Steve seemingly not used to walking more than about a hundred yards in one go, but they eventually got there.

The outside of the V Café was painted green, the sign proudly proclaiming it to be Mildenheath's first vegan restaurant.

'What the hell's this?' Steve said, trying to catch his breath.

'It's the restaurant,' Ryan replied, deadpan. 'You coming in?'

'What, to eat a plate of lentils and tofu? No thanks.'

'Alright. You'd better start walking back, then,' Ryan said. 'You might still have a few minutes left for a sandwich and a glass of water by the time you get back to the office. On the other hand, they do the best pineapple juice this side of Jamaica.'

Steve looked up at the restaurant again, then back down the hill towards the centre of Mildenheath.

'Might as well give it a go seeing as I'm here. But if they try any of that "meat is murder" shit, I'm off.'

Ryan smiled as she ushered Steve into the restaurant. Culverhouse walked in behind him, not saying a word, but at the same time not taking his eyes off Ryan.

Steve Wing and Jack Culverhouse sat at the table gingerly, as if it were made of plywood and liable to crack under their weight. They eyed the menu suspiciously, Culverhouse holding it pinched between his thumb and forefinger in one corner as though it were covered in something contagious.

'What the fuck's *quin-ower?*' he said after a few moments.

'It's pronounced *keen-wah*. It's quite nice, actually,' Wendy said.

Culverhouse glared at her.

'I can recommend the five bean burger,' Ryan chipped in. 'Really good with their guacamole.'

'Five. Bean. Burger,' Culverhouse said slowly, enunciating each word. 'A burger. Made of beans.'

'Well, it'd be a bit silly making it out of dead cow for a

vegan restaurant, wouldn't it?' Wendy said, not sure about the five bean burger herself, but keen to try and make Ryan feel as if she had an ally.

'See, that's what I don't understand,' Steve said, his eyebrows narrowed. 'If vegans hate meat, why do they insist on making vegetables look like meat? I mean, I'm not going to go around asking for a rasher of bacon in the shape of a lettuce leaf.'

'Have you ever tried putting a spoonful of beans inside a burger bun?' Ryan replied, silencing him.

Culverhouse let out a deep sigh. 'I suppose you're going to have a load of time off sick every few weeks, then, if you're one of these vegelesbians. You never see a healthy-looking one.'

Ryan smiled. 'I'm a vegan, not a vegetarian. And before you ask, yes I'm a lesbian.'

'Fuck me,' Culverhouse replied. 'Getting a full fucking house here, aren't we? Shame you're not black, or you'd've filled our quota for this year's intake on your own.'

'I know. But I can use a wheelchair if that'd help,' Ryan replied.

Culverhouse just raised his eyebrows.

'I presume you're the butch one,' Steve added, with all the tact and delicacy of a sledgehammer to the face. 'I mean, having a bloke's name and all.'

'I don't know. Why don't you ask my girlfriend, Thor?'

'Thor?'

'It's a joke, Steve. She's called Mandy.'

'That's a yes, then,' Culverhouse muttered under his breath.

'Right, well I think I know what I'm having,' Wendy said, keen to move the conversation on to less controversial topics. Since last night with Xav, she'd felt different, almost as if a weight had been lifted off her shoulders. She dared not say as much, but it was almost as if she'd begun to move on, started to see that it was possible to enjoy life and the company of men once again.

Well, some men at least.

22

From the restaurant, Wendy headed straight towards Milden-heath General Hospital. She wanted to get some more insight into the medical situation of Tanya Henderson — anything which could potentially help them with their inquiries.

Up on the ward, she found a very tired John Henderson sitting at his wife's bedside. The bags under his eyes were growing ever more pronounced.

'How are you holding up?' she asked him.

He forced a smile, one which didn't last very long before the muscles in his face succumbed once again to tiredness.

'Any news from the doctors?'

John shook his head. 'Nothing. Just seems to be a waiting game. How are the kids?'

'They're fine,' Wendy replied. 'The Aldridges are happy to keep an eye on them for as long as you'd like.'

'Thanks. If we had other family closer, we'd... Well, you know.'

'Don't worry about it. They seem like good people, your neighbours. You're lucky. Most people don't even know who their neighbours are.'

'Yeah. Well I just don't want the kids seeing Tanya like this. It's not fair on them.'

Wendy agreed. Seeing Tanya's battered and bruised body, her head partially shaved, all manner of wires and tubes sticking out of her — that wasn't something even an adult should see, let alone a small child. 'Have you eaten?' she asked him.

'Uh, yeah, a few hours ago probably.'

'Why don't you head down to the café and grab yourself something? You need to eat.'

'I'm not hungry,' he replied.

'But you need to eat. It's not going to do you any good to just sit here and look at her. It'll only take a few minutes. If there's any change, I promise I'll come and get you myself.'

'I'm fine. Honestly.'

Wendy could see there was very little point in arguing with him while he was so tired and in that frame of mind, so instead she smiled, rose, and headed for the nurse's station. When she got there, she was fortunate enough to be able to steal some time with the ward nurse, who was kind enough to offer Wendy fifteen minutes of her own lunch break.

'Has there been any news since we last spoke?' Wendy asked her.

'No, everything's still pretty stable. That's generally a good sign, although we'd obviously want to see signs of improvement. She seems to be coping well, though.'

'Well enough to be able to do it on her own?' Wendy asked, knowing that the only way they were going to make a real breakthrough on this case was if Tanya regained consciousness and was able to tell them who might have done this to her.

The nurse raised her eyebrows momentarily. 'It's entirely possible. You never know. The brain's a funny old thing. To be honest, the levels of intracranial pressure were on the high side of normal when she came in, but they haven't risen at all since then. If anything, they've dropped slightly.'

'That's a good sign, surely?' Wendy asked, wanting at least something to hold onto, at least some good news to tell Culverhouse.

'Yeah, absolutely. It's only one thing, though. There are a number of things we look at when we decide whether or not to induce a coma or to end an induced coma.'

'And, in your opinion, do you think she's close to being brought out of it?'

'In my opinion, yeah. I probably would've brought her out of it by now. Actually, to be honest, I probably wouldn't have induced it in the first place.'

'Really?'

'Yeah. I mean, obviously it's got its risks — any medical

procedure does — but on top of that, I wouldn't have said she was quite at that critical level. Then again, different doctors and different consultants have different views on these things. Some think you're better safe than sorry, and others like to allow the body to do its own thing. Medicine's a rich tapestry.'

Wendy smiled and nodded. 'A bit like policing, then.'

'I should imagine there are a lot of similarities,' the nurse replied, beaming. There was always an odd sense of inter-service camaraderie between the different areas of the public sector. Almost a unifying, defiant knowledge of what the other had to go through in order to simply do their job in modern times.

The door opened and the friendly face of Julian Mills, the consultant, peered round it. 'Alright if I come in?' he asked.

'Of course, no problem,' Wendy replied. 'We were just talking about Tanya Henderson. And about how long she's likely to be in the induced coma.'

'Ah, yes,' Mills said. 'Well, it's always a very delicate balancing act when we're talking about brain trauma. Personally, I like to make sure things are stabilised for a bit longer than usual before we take any drastic measures. A lot of the brain's healing is done over long periods of time, some of it years after the patient leaves the hospital. There's quite a bit of evidence to suggest that their long-term recovery can be sped up by a slightly increased period of medically induced coma. It's a bit like that extra half an hour in bed in the morning; it can give you a good couple of hours of extra time at the end of the day.'

'When you say slightly increased,' Wendy asked, 'how long are we actually talking?'

'Impossible to say,' the consultant replied. 'Sorry, I know that's not what you want to hear.'

'But she's stable at the moment, yes?'

'Yes, at the moment she is. Things can still change very quickly, though. Don't forget it's been barely thirty-six hours since the original trauma. There's still a lot of insta-bility under the surface. Things might be stable while she's in a medically induced coma, but bringing her out too early could reverse all the good that's been done.'

Wendy sighed and looked at the nurse, who took her unspoken cue to leave the room.

'The thing is,' Wendy continued, once she'd gone, 'we need to find out who did this. An innocent woman being attacked on her own front doorstep, with her four-year-old daughter watching.' She could see the empathy in Julian Mills's eyes. 'Do you have children?'

'Yes, two,' he replied.

'The problem we have is that the only direction we have to go in right now is that of Tanya's own witness testi-mony. Everything else leads us to a dead end. Without being able to speak to her to find out what she knows, I'm afraid it's looking extremely unlikely that we'll ever discover who did this. And bearing in mind there's a very high chance that Tanya's life and the lives of her children will be changed forever, and a half-decent chance that she might not recover at all... Well, would you want your kids to have to go through that? Never knowing why it happened or who did it?' Wendy stared at Julian's crestfallen face, knowing that she'd hit the right spot.

'Listen, there are always compromises that can be made. Like I said, it's still early days. But if she stays stable for the next few hours, I'm happy to look at starting to reduce the levels of barbiturates. If we see signs of deterioration, though, we'll have to increase the dose again. I want to help you as much as I can, of course, but I do need to put my patient's safety first.'

Wendy smiled. 'Thanks, doc.'

23

Jack Culverhouse closed the door to Charles Hawes's office behind him and walked back down the corridor. The Chief Constable was, to all intents and purposes, generally on his side, but it was hard not to feel the increasing weight of pressure on him, knowing that it was going to be all but impossible to find out who had attacked Tanya Henderson — not without her own witness testimony, at least, and there was a distinct and growing possibility that her testimony was something they were never going to get.

He didn't have too long to ponder the possibilities, however, as he was soon fishing his ringing mobile phone out of his jacket pocket. The display showed him it was Antonio García, calling from Spain. He swiped the screen to answer the call.

'Antonio,' he said, flatly.

'Jack. Why so cheery? Shit weather again?'

'Yeah, something like that,' Culverhouse replied, for once too exhausted to engage in the usual banter.

'Well, let's see. I've been doing a bit more work for you. You can buy me a few beers later. I think we're up to around one hundred,' García said, laughing. 'A guy I used to work with, Leandro Martín, now works privately. Cheating husbands, social security cheats, all that sort of thing. He owes me a favour too, so I mentioned you to him.'

'Oh, right,' Culverhouse replied, not quite sure how to take this.

'Jack, he's good. He has contacts. He had a tip-off from someone about a woman and her daughter in Redován. It's a town about twenty, twenty-five kilometres inland from Torrevieja. Listen. You mentioned a while back that your daughter Emily has a birthmark on the back of her neck, yes?'

Culverhouse swallowed. 'Yeah. Just behind her left ear. Why?'

'Because the girl Leandro's been watching has one too. We can't say anything for certain at the moment but, in Leandro's words, she certainly doesn't look Spanish. She has blonde hair.'

Culverhouse could feel his heart racing. Whenever he looked back and thought of Emily, it was her bright blonde hair he first saw, the light glistening off it as she played in the garden without a care in the world. Surely there were a number of blonde girls in Spain, so there was nothing yet to say this was Emily, but even the fact that there was the smallest chance it could be her — that kept him hanging on. It was the closest he'd come to finding her since she left. After the best part of a decade without any information, this was music to his ears.

'What about Helen? Is she with her?'

'There is a woman sometimes, yes. Her mother, it seems. That's what Leandro thinks, anyway. She has darker hair, cropped short. Wears glasses.'

It was possible it could be Helen. It didn't seem to match how she'd looked recently, but that didn't mean much. She only wore glasses occasionally, but it was entirely possible she'd wear them all the time now. And as for the hair, it would only have taken her an hour to get a new hairdo. That was perfectly feasible, particularly if she was looking to start a new life. The girl, on the other hand, sounded just like Emily.

'I need to tell you, Jack, it is very early days. Leandro has been trying to keep his distance, but has also been keeping an eye on them. That's not as easy as you might think, particularly not in this place where they're staying. But he has been doing his best. He sent me a photo. I'll email it to you now,' he said.

A few seconds later, Culverhouse's mobile pinged and vibrated in his ear.

'One sec,' he said, taking the phone from his ear and navigating through to his email inbox. After what seemed like an age, the email and the photo loaded. It had been taken from quite some distance, and the people in the image could have been anyone, but that was no bad thing as far as Jack was concerned. It meant it could also be

Helen and Emily. The older woman's face was obscured, but it was feasible it was Helen. As for the younger girl, Emily had been so young when he last saw her that he wondered if he would even recognise her walking down the street.

'What do you think?' García's voice said, tinny and distant as it came through the phone's earpiece.

Culverhouse put the phone back to his ear. 'I dunno. It's possible,' he said. 'I'll need a better picture before I can say for sure.'

'He's working on it,' García said. 'But it's not easy. Redován is a small place. You can't get up close and take a picture very easily. He can't even park too close to the house as everybody in the area will know if there is a strange car. He has to park on the adjacent street and use a long lens. It's difficult to get closer. We don't want to spook her.'

Culverhouse agreed. The last thing he wanted was for Helen and Emily to figure out what was going on and disappear into the ether again. 'Listen, send me the address,' he said.

'Jack, are you sure? It's—'

'Just send me the address. If it's them, it's best that I get out there and see them for myself. If I turn up, she's hardly likely to just run. She's come back twice already, so she's obviously open to speaking to me. But if she reckons your guys are government officials or police, we've lost them, particularly if she's been living off-radar all this time.'

'And if it's not them?'

'Then it won't make a blind bit of difference, will it? A strange Englishman turning up on their doorstep and saying "Sorry, wrong house"? What's the worst that can happen?'

García sighed. 'You tell me, Jack. You tell me.'

24

'Now, this is interesting...' Ryan said, when only Wendy was in earshot.

Wendy had only just returned from the hospital after speaking with Julian Mills, and had been hoping for a few minutes alone with a mug of coffee. 'What's that?' she replied, trying to sound as friendly and accommodating as possible.

'I've been reading up more on the past articles Tanya Henderson wrote, all these scandals and things she'd been investigating. The footballer, Callum Woods, the one she exposed for his addiction to prostitutes? Get this. There's a quote from him in a news article here: "When asked for his response, Woods had no comment to make on the allegations, only saying, 'This has ruined my family and affected my career. People never think of these things. How would this so-called journalist appreciate her whole life being ruined?' The footballer, who scored two goals in the..."

And it goes on. You get the picture. But what about that, eh?'

'Interesting,' Wendy said. 'What, you reckon it was a direct threat?'

'I dunno. Sounds to me like the paper called him up for a comment and he was too livid to even realise what he was saying. It's an old CIA technique from the States. Get them cornered and flustered, and they'll say all sorts. They're too busy worrying about what could go wrong to even think about what they're saying at the time. And that's when the real person comes out.'

Wendy pursed her lips. 'Could be something in it. But what are we saying? That this Callum Woods attacked Tanya?'

Ryan winked at Wendy. 'I'm not saying anything. Only that it might be worth speaking to him and finding out a bit more. I mean, think about it. This guy's earning tens of thousands a week. He's married with kids, and he's going around having his wicked way with sex workers. His wife's not going to be keen on that. His teammates probably aren't going to respond all that well, either.'

'Oh come on,' Wendy said. 'You think they're not all at it?'

'Possibly. But then there's the crowds, too. The supporters. Footballers are role models these days. Callum Woods was being touted for an England call up just a few days before that story broke. That was a year ago, and he's still not played for them. His whole career seems to have been put on pause. It's only recently that he's started picking up form on the pitch again, apparently.'

'But why wait a year? Why do something stupid like this now, when things are just starting to pick up again for him? If he was going to attack her, wouldn't he have done it months ago? When the pain was still fresh?'

Ryan shrugged. 'Who knows? Footballers are hardly known for their brains, are they? Got to be worth speaking to him at least.'

'We'll need to get Culverhouse's approval. Where is he?'

'No idea,' Ryan replied.

'Anyone seen the guv?' Wendy called to the rest of the room.

'I think he went to see the Chief Constable,' Steve Wing said. 'I wouldn't want to disturb them if I were you. I'd probably give it an hour after he gets out, too. Make sure all the steam's gone out of his ears first.'

Wendy turned back to Ryan. 'Where's this Callum Woods live?'

'Not sure. I'd imagine somewhere in the East Midlands, looking at who he plays for. I can give the club a ring and see if they'll give us his home address. Either that or get the local force to find it for us. But that might be a bit official.'

Wendy agreed. 'True. Last thing we want is to give the guy any more bad publicity, especially if he's innocent. I tell you what. Find out who his agent is and get in touch with him. That's got to be the best way. It'll be in the

agent's best interest that he cooperates with us for the sake
of his client, and he'll want to keep it on the hush-hush too,
for obvious reasons.'

'Good idea. I'll get onto it.'

'Here we are,' Frank Vine said, as he put down the
phone. 'Confirmation from the science bods. The weapon
used was a crowbar, they reckon. One of the new stainless
steel ones. They reckon if it was one of the old powder-
coated ones there'd be traces of paint or something.'

'Good. Nice one, Frank. Now we need to get onto local
retail outlets and see if we can find out who bought a
crowbar there recently. In the last month, perhaps.'

'Seriously?' Frank asked, raising an eyebrow. 'I mean,
I'm not being funny but what does a crowbar cost? A fiver?
Tenner? Whoever it was will've paid in cash.'

'Then with any luck they'll be on CCTV somewhere.
Most shops will have itemised tills, so they'll be able to drill
down to when any crowbars were sold. Maybe get onto the
online retailers and the big chains, too, see if any were
ordered for home delivery within a twenty-mile radius over
the past month.'

'Might want to check Callum Woods's garage, too,'
Ryan quipped.

Frank made a quiet snort of derision. 'That useless
twat couldn't hit a barn door with a banjo, never mind a
woman's head with a crowbar.'

Turning to Ryan, Wendy lowered her voice.
'Depending on how Callum Woods appears when we
speak to him, we might want to take a closer look at his

records, too. Bank and credit card statements, phone bills, all that sort of thing. Even if he's involved, it's highly unlikely he'll have done it himself. Actually,' she said, turning back to the others, 'do we have any news on Tanya Henderson's call logs?'

'Nope, just the silent call a minute or so before she was attacked. Came from an unregistered pay-as-you-go mobile, in the vicinity of the IP's house. Never been switched on or used before then.'

'Nothing in the texts or other phone calls?'

'Nothing of interest, no. Just calls to and from the office.'

Wendy sighed. The likelihood was that Tanya Henderson had all her conversations in person, one-to-one. Everything was kept off the record.

Being security-conscious was one thing, but in Tanya Henderson's case it had proven to be more of a hindrance than a help.

25

Culverhouse hated airports at the best of times. They were always either full of people happy to be going on holiday, or miserable at having to go away for work or return home for a family funeral. He certainly wasn't going on holiday, but he didn't want to be surrounded by a bunch of miserable bastards either.

The departures information board showed him that the flight to Alicante was due to leave in two hours. He'd packed light — hand luggage only, as he didn't know how long he was going to be staying. If García's contact had been wrong, he'd be in and out within a few hours. If he needed to stay longer, well, he'd taken plenty of cash and credit cards. He'd be able to buy anything he needed while he was over there.

He'd tried to speak to Charles Hawes after the call with García, but he hadn't been in his office, and having looked up the next flights to Alicante, he certainly wasn't going to hang around to ask for permission. Sometimes, things were more important than work. Hawes would understand. He'd have to. And if he didn't, tough. Culverhouse could feel himself being squeezed out of the job from either side as it was. If he managed to find Emily, they could shove the job. Let the bastards win. He wouldn't care. As long as he found Emily.

The newsagents and duty-free shops were mobbed with people wheeling suitcases around, picking up copies of newspapers they never usually read and bottles of perfume they'd never usually buy. An announcement on the loudspeaker called for a passenger on the Krakow flight to return to the check-in desk as quickly as possible. All these people, going to all these places, all over the world. It was as if the whole of the planet's population had been distilled down into this small representative sample. Even with that, however, the place was still overrun with bald-headed beer-bellied blokes in England shirts, getting tanked up ready for their week in Benidorm. Culverhouse made a note to apologise on behalf of his country while he was over there.

He went into the newsagent and bought himself a copy of a newspaper he'd never usually read. It was a way to pass the time, he supposed. He flicked through the pages absentmindedly, his eyes scanning over stories of wars in the middle east, corruption in American politics, scandals in sport. It was all doom and gloom. It was one of the reasons why he never usually read newspapers. Surely some good things must be happening in the world? Apparently not.

Instead, he decided to buy a book — the travel diaries of some bloke he'd never heard of — and managed to lose himself in it for the best part of an hour, before realising that the coffee he'd ordered had gone cold. He looked at the drink and grunted, before getting up and heading for the security area.

It was a good half an hour before he finally got through security, having put his belt back on, re-tied his shoes and filled his pockets back up with all of the things they were filled with that he probably didn't need. The departures information board told him the flight to Alicante was now boarding, so he headed for gate twenty-one as indicated.

The number of people queuing at the gate seemed enormous. How could that many people possibly fit onto a plane? The truth of the matter was that most of them were probably heading off for a week's holiday, or perhaps even going out to their second home. Jack definitely needed a piece of that; he couldn't remember the last time he'd gone on holiday. Certainly not since Helen had left, anyway.

He wondered momentarily if it was worth it. What was he doing this for? Was it for Emily or for himself? He wasn't entirely sure, but in his heart of hearts he really thought it was for Emily. Before now, he hadn't done half as much as he could've done to try and find them. But that's because he knew he wouldn't be a good father. He knew Emily would be better off with Helen, better off away from the poison that was having a father in the police force. A father who left in the early hours and came back in the even earlier hours. A father who could only ever see bad in people. Emily deserved more than that.

Since Helen had returned, though, his thoughts had changed slightly. Emily still deserved the best, but Jack was becoming less and less sure that the best option was for her to be with Helen. It wasn't just the fact that she'd developed a mental illness — although that did play a part — but he could also see how much Helen had fallen apart over the years. She wasn't the strong, confident woman he remembered.

Before she'd returned, Jack was certain that Emily was safe with Helen. If anyone could cope with leaving the country and raising a child on their own, Helen could. That's what he'd thought back then. Now, though, he doubted it gravely.

Emily was at that age now where she was becoming extremely impressionable. The early teens were hell for any parent, but a single mother living in a foreign land with a mental illness surely had to raise a few eyebrows. In Jack's case, it was more that he was worried for the future of his daughter. He knew how easily influenced young adults were. He saw it all the time. He could predict with remarkable accuracy which twelve- and thirteen-year-olds in Mildenheath would be in prison before their twenty-first birthdays. Forward planning, he called it. He didn't want Emily to be one of those.

The queue seemed to be taking an age to move forward, but Jack now had only three people in front of him. Within a few minutes they'd be in the air and he'd be on his way to potentially see his daughter for the first time in nine years. No more putting work first. This was it: time for him and her. Together.

His phone started to vibrate in his pocket, so he fished his hand in and pulled it out. It was DC Debbie Weston's direct dial number.

'Debbie, what is it? I can't really talk right now.'

'It's Tanya Henderson, guv. She's woken up.'

26

The sounds are clearer, richer. The words are beginning to make sense. I can feel my heart rate increasing, sense the first surge of adrenaline.

Then I slip behind again, the fog and the fuzz overtaking me. I try to hold on, try to clear the mist, and this time I'm successful.

The noises are loud, almost painful. Every sound vibrates and rings in my ears.

I think I've been awake for some time, but I'm not really sure what awake means. I think I'm conscious, but I still struggle to will myself to do the things I want to do.

It sounds strange, but I don't even know if my eyes are open. It's difficult to tell. I don't even know what vision is. I've seen things — crisp, clear images — but I know I wasn't actually seeing them. It's like those first few seconds after waking up from a vivid dream, not quite knowing which reality is real. It's a state of perpetual confusion, your brain telling you one thing and showing you another.

The light begins to burn. It's not a light that suddenly appears; it seems as though it's been there all along, but it's only just started to seep through, only just started to burn. It's another level of increasing awareness, as if different areas of my brain are slowly unlocking. It's like walking around the house first thing in the morning and drawing all of the curtains. Each drawn curtain lets in more light, allows you to see more of the outside world.

I feel a gasp rising from my lungs, can hear it as it escapes my lips.

I become aware of my own breathing, aware of it increasing in speed.

I hear voices. No meaning. Just words.

I start to pick out a sense of what those words mean. The confusion tries to take over, but I fight it back.

I hear a word and I know immediately what it means.

'Tanya?'

It's a word full of meaning. A word which anchors me in the here and now. Something for me to grasp onto. Something for me to use.

'Tanya?'

I feel a hand on my wrist. It's calm, reassuring. I don't know whose it is, but I like it. It comforts me.

The words begin to echo and fade, before conglomerating into a roaring noise. It crescendoes, with a crystal clear silence lingering afterwards. Then I hear the words again, this time soft, distinct.

'Everything is okay, Tanya. Try to breathe slowly. You're doing just fine.' The voice is soothing. I recognise the accent. It's a soft Scottish lilt. 'Tanya, do you know where you are?'

I hear another voice. One I recognise. 'Can we give her a few minutes? Do the questioning after?'

The Scottish voice speaks again, this time quietly, addressing the voice I now recognise as John's. 'It's a fairly lengthy process, Mr Henderson. We need to test a range of stimuli both immediately after she wakes up and then throughout the following hours and days.'

All of these words make sense to me, but not in this situation. Why are they talking in this way? Are they talking about me?

'Do you know where you are, Tanya?' the Scottish voice asks again.

I try to speak, but I can't. My chest burns with the effort. I try to shake my head, slowly. I don't know if I'm succeeding, but my neck creaks and groans, the shockwaves vibrating up through my skull. I manage to force a half-groan, half-whisper.

'No...'

'You're in Mildenheath General Hospital, Tanya. Don't worry, though. You're going to be alright. There was an incident and you were hurt, but you're doing fine. Do you remember what happened?'

I try to take another breath, before repeating the same word.

'No...'

There's a pause. 'Okay. Try not to worry too much. Tanya, can you tell me how old you are?'

I know this answer instinctively.

'Thirty-five.'

The words seem to take an age to leave my lips. My voice sounds raspy.

'And where do you live, Tanya? Which house number?'

'Manor Way. Twenty-three.'

'That's great. Well done. Do you remember anything about what happened the other night? About the incident?'

I try to force myself to remember. I know I need to. But there's nothing. I can't even identify the last thing I do remember.

I try to shake my head again, but it hurts.

'No.'

'Okay,' the voice says. 'We can come back to that.'

'What about work? Do you remember what you were working on?' The voice is John's.

I don't. I don't remember anything. I know it was important. Big. Huge. But it feels like the more importance I attach to it, the less my brain is letting me remember.

'No.'

'You need to try to remember, Tanya. Can you remember anything? Names? Locations? Anything.'

I can't. I can't. I'm trying, but I can't.

'No...' I say.

I hear a female voice. 'Her heart rate and breathing are increasing.'

'It's okay, Tanya. Not to worry. You stay relaxed. Breathe slowly,' says the Scottish voice. 'I think we should leave it there for the moment.'

The reassuring hand on my wrist squeezes me tighter, before letting go.

27

Frank Vine opened the car door, stepped out and grimaced as he plunged his hand into his pocket, jangling a collection of loose change.

'Bloody scandalous, this is. Three quid a pop just to do my own job.'

Using his thumb, he shoved four coins into the coin slot, then jabbed the green button on the parking ticket dispenser.

'Put it on expenses,' Wendy said, closing the passenger door behind her as she got out of the car.

'If you think I'm going to spend forty-five minutes filling out a bloody document just to get three quid back a month later, you're having a laugh.'

Frank slapped the ticket on his dashboard, slammed the car door shut, and started to march towards the hospital, Wendy trying her best to keep up with him.

Inside, they made their way to the specialist brain

injury unit, where they were met by Julian Mills, who took them into a side room.

'Right. The good news is Tanya's regained consciousness. From a medical point of view, that is. I think it's fair to say she's not up and dancing about just yet, but as far as medicine is concerned, she's fully conscious.'

'Is she talking?' Frank asked.

'To a degree, yes. She's finding speech difficult, but that's to be expected.'

'And is that because of the injury?' Wendy said.

'Difficult to say at this stage. It could be to do with the injury, or it could just be because of the amount of time she's been unconscious. The drugs could play a part, too. She's been through a hell of a lot these past couple of days. We're going to do some more tests throughout the day, which'll include testing her nerve responses and motor skills. We'll know more then.'

'What are we looking at?' Frank asked. 'Worst case scenario, I mean.'

The consultant sighed. 'Well, I think we all know what the worst case scenario is; just because she's conscious and communicating now doesn't mean that'll always be the case. You never know with the brain. All we can do is start to approach an increasing degree of certainty as more time passes. Long-term, we could be looking at impaired movement and balance, development of dyspraxia or apraxia, sensory deficits, behavioural changes, cognitive issues... The list really does go on and on.'

'What kind of behavioural changes?' Wendy asked.

The consultant smiled. 'Like I say, you never know with the brain. It's a very delicate but quite extraordinary piece of machinery. I've seen people with horrendous brain injuries go on to live perfectly normal lives, much as they did before their injury. And I've seen people with relatively minor injuries have their lives completely turned upside down.'

'How so?'

'Well, anything from complete physical paralysis to what might seem to be a completely new personality. Different parts of the brain switch off or activate as they or other parts are irreparably injured. We think that even the brain repairing itself can sometimes cause short circuits, if you like, which can lead to some strange things happening. I remember one case,' he said, sitting down on the arm of a sofa, 'in which one young man — he can't have been more than twenty — was in a motorbike accident. He was wearing a helmet, and the accident was pretty minor, really. But the effect on his life was incredible. Within a week he'd left his partner and their young son, quit his job and turned to heavy drugs. Before that he'd been a doting young father coming to the end of his apprenticeship. All that because of a relatively minor bump on the head.' He shrugged, as though he were saying "that's life".

Wendy didn't quite know what to say to this. It was the unpredictability of the whole situation that depressed her — the not knowing. In her job she was used to often being one step behind, having to play constant catch-up with whoever they were seeking, but this time it was different.

There was nothing they could do until they knew what Tanya Henderson's situation was going to be.

'Now, in my expert opinion, I would say it looks as though Tanya's quite confused,' Mills said. 'That's to be expected, though, after what she's been through. Her brain is still trying to repair itself. One minute she was sitting at her desk, and the next she's waking up in hospital two days later, surrounded by police. The brain will do all sorts of things to make sense of that. After I had the nurse call you, I spoke to Tanya some more. Nothing official, and no specific tests as such, but just to get an idea of how her mind was working and to observe how she was doing. There were one or two things that gave me some cause for concern, but nothing too major.'

'Like what?' Frank asked.

'I really wouldn't worry too much,' the consultant replied, waving his hand. 'It's quite a common thing. I had one patient a few months back, who for the first week and a half he was here swore blind he was Elvis, risen from the dead. I'm sure it'll pass.'

Wendy's heart sank. Even if Tanya Henderson were to remember something — or to think she remembered something — how reliable would that information actually be? The likelihood of any of it standing up in court would be extremely low, particularly if no hard, incontrovertible evidence was there to accompany it.

There had been a police presence on the ward ever since Tanya Henderson had been admitted — that much had been decreed by Culverhouse when it became clear she would likely still be a target for whoever had attacked her in the first place. Wendy was satisfied that Tanya Henderson was safe — for now, at least — but what would happen if she were to be in a fit enough state to be discharged from hospital? And what if she was unable to provide them with any further information? Not only would they not be able to get any closer to finding whoever had done this to her, but they'd also find it far more difficult to protect her from that person.

Wendy knew that time was against them. But she didn't know how little time they had left.

28

Culverhouse struggled to regain his breath as he clambered into the taxi and put on his seatbelt.

His head was a mess. Half an hour earlier he'd been ready to board a flight to Alicante to see his daughter for the first time in nine years. A couple of hours before that he'd been sitting in the Chief Constable's office. And now he was in the back of a cab, on his way back to Mildenheath CID, a broken and confused man.

He couldn't make any sense of his thoughts. He'd had no choice: he was damned if he did and damned if he didn't. But he couldn't help that overriding feeling of guilt, the realisation that he'd done it again. As always, the job had got in the way. And, as always, he'd sat back and succumbed to the job, letting Emily down yet again. This time, she wouldn't even know it. He wondered how much she really *did* know. Whether she even knew his name.

That was the hardest part of it all. Jack liked to plan

ahead, to always keep a few steps ahead of the game, but in this situation he was no longer in control. He never *had* been in control. And that was a problem — a big one.

He pulled his mobile phone out of his pocket, unlocked the screen, and immediately forgot what he was about to do. Clenching his teeth, he pummelled the heel of his hand into the side of his head three times before he remembered. Going into his contacts list, he tapped Antonio García's name.

The phone seemed to take an age to connect, the lonely silence making him feel more and more agitated until the cross-border connection was finally made and the low ringing sound started in his ear.

'Jack! Where are you? Was your flight delayed?' came the answer once the call had connected.

Culverhouse exhaled. He wanted to cry. 'Something like that. Listen, I won't be coming out today. Something's come up. Something important.'

'More important?' García asked.

Culverhouse never realised how quickly he could go from wanting to cry to wanting to rip someone's head off. He found himself struggling for words. He wanted to tell Antonio that no, nothing was more important to him than his daughter. He wanted to tell him that he had no choice, that he was wedded to the job. He wanted to tell him that he'd done a stupid, terrible thing and that he should be on that plane right now and fuck the lot of them. But no words came.

'Jack? What's happened?'

He paused for a moment. 'Nothing. Probably nothing. Can you just... Can you ask your man to hold tight? Keep an eye on them. See what you can find out. I'll be there. I will. Just not today.'

He could almost hear García smiling at the other end of the phone. 'Of course. Don't worry.'

'I mean, I'll cover their costs. I'll pay them. Whatever it is, I'll pay it. Just... I can't be there right now.'

'Jack, don't worry,' García repeated. 'And there is no cost. They owe me a favour, I told you. They owe me more than a favour, actually, but that's another story for another day. Listen, I understand. There are hundreds of flights to Alicante. We won't be going anywhere. When you are able to come out, come out.'

'Thanks,' Culverhouse replied, unable to say any more. He terminated the call.

The buildings and parked cars whizzed past the window as he gazed out, focusing on nothing much at all. He wasn't thinking of much at all, either.

He gladly let his mind wander into nothingness, the noise of his thoughts fading into the background as he tried to let everything go.

29

I've got a headache. And that's putting it lightly. The doctors say the painkillers will be taking the worst of it away, but it feels like it's not even touching the sides. The medication just makes me feel drowsy. I don't know how much of that is down to the barbiturates they had me on to keep me comatose, but all I know is I don't feel like me.

I still feel detached, spaced out. Almost as if I'm watching this rather than taking part in it. It's a very odd sensation, and not one I can accurately describe.

The doctors keep coming in and asking me odd questions. I can see what they're doing — they're testing my long-term and short-term memory. They'll come in and ask me something, then have a chat, then ask me the same question again. They'll ask me who the prime minister is, what year I was born, what their own names are. They'll ask me to work out maths problems and to read charts of letters like they have at the optician's.

That's the hardest part for me. The letter charts. My vision's still incredibly blurred. The doctors say there's some swelling on the back of my brain, around the optic nerve. Papilledema, they call it. See. I remembered that.

There are definitely holes, though. Fortunately they've not been able to find them yet. I hope to keep it like that, so they'll let me go home sooner rather than later.

John, for example. He's here, next to me, most of the time. I hear his voice, and I can see him there, but not distinctly. My vision's still too blurred. But the most disturbing thing is that I can't remember his face.

When I first realised that, my heart sank. What if I never regain my vision? The doctors tell me I will. They assure me it's just down to the swelling. The papilledema. But the fact that I can't even visualise my own husband's face from memory frightens the hell out of me. I remember the day we met, the day we married, the day our children were born. But I can't remember his face. In every image, every memory reel I have in my mind, his face is the same indistinct blur of colour I see in front of me now. That terrifies me.

To be honest, this whole place scares me. I feel distinctly uncomfortable here, but I can't put my finger on why. It's probably because I've never liked hospitals. Horrible places. Who likes being in hospital? No-one. I want to get out, get back home, get back to work.

Work. There's a word. It's a huge, missing chunk. In my mind, I can visualise my study at home, the room where I do most of my work. At least I think I can visualise it. I can visualise most of my house, but there are bits missing. Then there are rooms that I'm certain exist but that don't seem to fit in with the floor plan I remember. I know, for example, that I don't have two living rooms. I know that instinctively, yet in my mind I see two, as clear as day.

My vision of my study is much clearer. Clearer than any other room. I can see it quite distinctly. The shelves of books, the filing cabinet, the desk. And I know I was working on something important. I'm always working on something important. What I do is important.

But that's as far as I get.

The more I try to think of it, the fuzzier everything becomes. It's like telling a naughty child to stop tapping their pencil on the side of the table. The more you tell them not to do it, the more they're going to do it.

I try to let my brain relax. Try to think of other things. My children. Archie and Lola. I can see their faces as clear as day, smiling and beaming. I'll never forget those faces. They're everything. It seems as though I can remember every single day of their lives. It's all there, crystal clear, brighter than anything.

Pevensey Park.

Those two words flash into my head like a bolt of lightning. I see them at the same time as I remember them, the words appearing in front of my eyes, as if on a computer screen. And then they disappear again.

In that moment, I realise their significance. I know how important they are. I know they're the key to this whole thing. I just don't know how or why.

Pevensey Park.

I try to say the words, but I don't know if they're leaving my lips. I can't hear them.

Pevensey Park.

The confusion starts to swamp me again. I feel my heart racing, my breath quickening. I groan as I try to sit up in bed. I feel a hand on my arm, holding me back. I want to call out, want to scream but I can't. I'm panicking.

My vision becomes more blurred. Colours appear, bright colours, flashes of light.

I don't know how much time has passed.

I hear voices.

More voices. The words become more indistinct.

I hear a humming.

Everything fades to blue.

30

'Well no, I wouldn't necessarily describe it as normal, but it is certainly something I've seen happen before,' Julian Mills said to Jack and Wendy outside the ward. Frank had been sent back to the office once Culverhouse had arrived, much to his chagrin. 'This is what I warned you about. It might seem as though someone is recovering well, but the brain is extraordinarily delicate in these situations. Any sort of stress or agitation can result in massively increased brainwave activity, which in turn can cause an increase of pressure on the brain. After what Tanya's already been through, it could be fatal.'

'How much did the pressure increase?' Wendy asked. 'Was it dangerously high?'

'It doesn't increase immediately,' the consultant replied. 'It doesn't take long for it to start, though, and with her levels of agitation and her increased heart rate and breathing, we weren't going to take any risks. We increased the dose of barbiturates to keep her sedated and mitigate the chances of a recurrence of the brain swelling. I'm not in the business of putting my patients in danger, I'm afraid.' Wendy could almost hear the doctor's silent end to that sentence: "no matter how much you need her to talk." He was probably annoyed at police officers getting in his way.

Wendy could feel her frustration starting to boil over. They had barely been off the ward for two or three minutes before returning to the news of Tanya's regression. 'Annoyed' didn't even cover it, but she was trying to bottle it up. By the time Wendy got even mildly frustrated, Culverhouse had usually blown his lid, but as she looked over at him, she saw him nodding slowly in acceptance of what the doctor was saying, calm as ever. She couldn't even be completely certain he was listening. He just seemed dazed, not with it at all.

'So we're back at square one?' Culverhouse asked, proving her wrong.

'Well, I wouldn't necessarily go that far,' the consultant replied. 'But it's definitely a step backwards. Hopefully it'll be a case of one step back, two steps forward, but what it does show is that Tanya's nowhere near being at a point where we can consider her to be better. I'm afraid it all seems to be a bit much for her at the moment. She's clearly in a very fragile state and was woken too soon. She needs time and space to recover, and the added pressure of a police presence is very unlikely to help,' he added, almost reluctantly, making Wendy think her hunch was correct.

'With all due respect, we need to find out who did this to her. This is looking like a case of attempted murder,' she said.

Julian Mills sighed. 'All I can say is that if you rush these things and put her under unnecessary strain, you certainly won't have a case of attempted murder. You'll have a case of murder. In which case, she won't be able to tell you a thing. I'm sorry, but we could have come close to losing her in there. I don't want that on my conscience and I'm fairly sure you don't, either.'

'But we need some form of police presence,' Wendy said. 'She's a target for someone. Someone tried to kill her and there's a good chance they'll try again.'

'Not in here, they won't. We already have very good security. Listen, I'm happy for you to continue to station an officer outside the ward, but not somewhere she can see them. If she remains stabilised and we wake her up again, we don't want her getting distressed. I'm happy for someone to be here for security purposes, but not for putting her under stress with questioning.'

Wendy nodded. 'That's fair enough. Is there anything else you can tell us?'

'Such as?'

'I don't know. How long it might be before you can bring her round again? How long after that it'll be before we can speak to her? Whether what happened in there earlier could cause any long-term damage?'

The consultant shrugged. 'Who knows? Right now we're back to playing the waiting game.'

Wendy sighed. She hated that game.

31

The evening light began to fade at about the same time as the large glass of whisky started to take the edge off Jack Culverhouse's mood. *It never rains, but it pours.* That was never truer than it was in the case of CID officers. There were times when he'd go weeks, months perhaps, without anything juicier than a fraud case or a gang-related assault to get his teeth into. His personal life would be just as quiet, too, with little more than the regular nine to five followed by a few episodes of *Breaking Bad* in the evening.

But Jack had never been a nine to five sort of person, and as much as he liked *Breaking Bad*, he was far happier doing the job he loved. The overtime wasn't as ubiquitous as it used to be, however, and he often found himself having to spend far too many evenings in his own company.

There were times when he didn't mind that so much, but those times were few and far between. His problem had always been that he was a thinker — indeed, he'd been guilty on many occasions of overthinking things. One of the downsides of the job was that his brain had been trained to consider every possibility and to always expect the worst. Overanalysis of one's personal life, though, was never ideal.

Try as he might, he couldn't shake the regrets. He knew he had a reputation as a hard-nosed bastard, and it was a reputation he was happy to have, but even Jack Culverhouse had regrets. Plenty of them.

He took another large gulp of whisky, feeling the ice cube chill his upper lip before holding the glass in his hand and swirling the amber liquid around, watching the melting ice infuse with it, marbling the liquor.

He could easily get a cab to the airport and book himself on the next flight to Alicante. The local airport had three flights a day going out at this time of year, and another hour's drive would open him up to a further three airports. But that wasn't what was stopping him.

True enough, when he'd been in that queue at the airport he'd had every intention of getting on that plane. Emily came first, and that's all there was to it. Then he'd received the phone call.

It was his reaction that had shocked him. His first instinct should've been to delegate, to tell them he'd be back in a couple of days and someone else would have to deal with it in the meantime. His daughter needed him. But that wasn't his first instinct. Not at all. The first thought that had crossed his mind was to head back out through security and get a cab back to the office. It was second nature to him now; a nature he wasn't sure how to break.

It wasn't that he wanted to go back to the office. It wasn't that he wanted to let Emily down again. It was the fact that it had been the first thing to cross his mind. His instinctive reaction. In that moment he'd realised that deep down he was still the same old Jack Culverhouse. That even if he went over to Spain, even if he got there and found out it was Emily, and even if she accepted him and became a part of his life again, he'd still find a way to let her down. He had just about learned to control his conscious reactions and thoughts, but he now realised that he couldn't control his subconscious impulses. And for as long as that was true, he couldn't trust himself.

He'd already blown it once, and he didn't deserve a second chance. But, if he ever somehow managed to get one, he sure as hell wasn't going to blow that too.

He'd never felt so disappointed in himself.

He thought about Tanya Henderson's children, Archie and Lola. There was a decent chance they'd lose their mother. A woman who doted on her kids, who tried to give them the very best in life. A woman who dedicated her life not only to her children but to exposing some of the worst forms of corruption in our society.

And then he compared her to himself. A bloke who couldn't even get home from work early enough to spend some time with his daughter. Who allowed his job to ride roughshod over his marriage and his family life. Who wouldn't know what being a good parent meant if it was drawn out on a piece of paper in front of him. Who was, shamefully, still alive.

It shouldn't be Tanya Henderson in that hospital bed, he thought. It should be him. Tanya Henderson should be at home with her kids, tucking them in and reading them a bedtime story. She deserved that. Her kids deserved that. And while she was lying there in that hospital bed, he had been getting ready to fly halfway across Europe on a whim to try and track down the daughter he didn't deserve.

Not for the first time in his life, Jack Culverhouse realised there was no justice in the world.

32

The dawn of a new day often brought new hope, but that morning was different. The investigation seemed to be stalling again. The inquiries into the purchase of crowbars in the local area hadn't thrown up anything particularly useful, and there were certainly no names coming up that were either known to the police or connected with Tanya Henderson. Without going out and speaking to each one of the purchasers individually — which might well have to be their next move — there wasn't a whole lot they could do.

Their main lead right now was Callum Woods. Wendy thought back to what seemed to be a thinly-veiled threat in his quote for the newspaper. It wouldn't be enough to stand up in court, but it was certainly well worth looking into, especially as they didn't currently have any other options.

Wendy wasn't particularly a football fan, but she'd been reading up about Woods and had familiarised herself with his various misdemeanours — or what the newspapers had seen fit to report on, anyway. Apart from the story about him regularly seeking the company of prostitutes — something Wendy vaguely recalled seeing in the newspapers just over a year ago — Callum Woods had been no stranger to media attention. From what she could garner, he'd never quite managed to live up to his off-field reputation on the football pitch itself. He'd come close a few times, and, as Ryan had told her, he was seemingly on the verge of an England call-up when the prostitute story broke. It seemed as though he'd been working hard to clean up his image, but had fallen at the last hurdle.

He'd first hit the headlines when he got involved in a drunken brawl outside a nightclub when he was just eighteen and had recently broken into his club's first team. He'd managed to avoid a prison sentence as the judge decided he had acted in self-defence, but the man he'd punched had ended up needing a metal plate in his jaw. *Liable to turn violent when threatened*, Wendy noted at the back of her mind.

It wasn't just his actions that had let Callum Woods down over the years, either. He'd been involved in a number of very public Twitter disputes with just about anyone who dared to criticise his form on the pitch, and had referred to a well-respected female daytime TV presenter as a 'sour old fishwife who probably hasn't had any for years' when she called him out on his behaviour.

Overall, it seemed that he'd become the epitome of the spoilt young rich kid, becoming far too famous far too young, before he'd even come to realise what the world was all about. It was something that was seen far too often, particularly amongst footballers and the world of the overnight celebrities who find themselves famous for absolutely no reason at all.

Wendy and Ryan headed over to his place, soon finding out that Callum Woods's house spoke for itself. A twenty-four-year-old with two children, he was living in what could only be described as a mansion.

'Bloody hell. We're in the wrong job,' Ryan said as Wendy parked the car up outside the front of the building, the tyres crunching along the gravel drive as she did so.

'Possibly, although I don't think the two of us would pass for Premier League footballers,' Wendy replied, a small smile playing on her lips.

They'd called ahead to Woods's agent, in order to make sure he'd be at home, and they'd managed to be relatively evasive about what the visit was about, which was always a good thing. It would give any potentially guilty parties far less time to prepare their excuses or alibis.

The front door opened before Wendy and Ryan had even got to it, and Wendy recognised Callum Woods immediately from the photos she'd seen online.

'Hi. Come in, come in,' he said, standing aside and waving them in. 'Sorry,' he said once he'd closed the door behind them. 'Can't be too careful. Not when it comes to the press. Thanks for not turning up in a marked car, by the way.'

'We're CID. We don't use marked cars,' Wendy

replied. 'You must get a lot of press intrusion, then?'

Callum replied as he led them through to the kitchen. 'You don't know the half of it. I've had them going through my bins before now. Any tiny little thing they can use and latch on to, they will. One women's magazine a few months ago even ran a feature about breastfeeding, and they absolutely bloody slaughtered us for feeding our kids formula milk rather than breast milk. All because they found the empty packaging from some formula in my bins. Funny thing is, it was my sister's. She'd been over with her two baby twins. Get this — my youngest kid was two-and-a-half at the time. Didn't even cross their minds that he might be on solids by now. Bloody parasites, the lot of them.'

Wendy couldn't disagree that there were elements of the gutter press that infuriated her, and in this instance she definitely agreed with him, but it was also fair to say that Callum Woods had probably deserved a fair bit of the negative publicity he'd had. After all, he'd put himself up on a pedestal and he'd blown it — he'd hardly been the best behaved person in the world.

'Goes with the job, I guess,' Ryan said to him.

He turned away slightly, though Wendy could still see the look on his face. It was obviously a line he'd heard a thousand times before, and it was one he patently didn't agree with. She could also see that Ryan knew this all too well, and had probably said it deliberately to get that exact reaction from him. Ryan was clearly the sort of officer who could go far. If certain people would let her, that was.

'Well, it's not quite that simple,' Woods replied after a moment. Wendy noted that he hadn't offered either of them a drink. 'So, what can I help you with?'

'It's with regards to an incident that happened in Mildenheath recently,' Ryan replied. Wendy had decided to let Ryan take the lead on this one. She seemed more than capable, and Wendy would be there to step in should anything happen. It also meant she could keep an eye on Woods, could look out for any sign that he might become violent.

'Mildenheath? Never heard of it.'

Ryan chose not to rise to the bait. 'It's to do with a woman called Tanya Henderson. Does the name ring a bell at all?'

Wendy could swear she saw the faintest glimmer of recognition in Woods's eyes. It was barely perceptible, but to the trained intuition of an experienced detective, it was definitely there.

'Sounds familiar, but I don't know why,' Woods replied, sitting down at the large, ornate kitchen dining table. Wendy and Ryan stayed standing. It's not like he'd invited them to sit, anyway.

'She's the journalist who broke the news story about your visits to prostitutes.'

'Is she? Yes, if you say so.' His face remained blank.

'Bit strange that you'd not remember her name, isn't it?' Ryan asked. 'Especially as she's the woman who nearly ruined your career.'

Woods laughed. 'I wouldn't go that far. I mean, it

wasn't ideal, but I can tell you now it'd take a lot more than a newspaper article to ruin my career.'

Taking a piece of paper from her pocket, Ryan read directly from the article. '"This has ruined my family and affected my career. People never think of these things."' She looked down at him.

'Yeah, and? People say things in the heat of the moment. And newspapers don't always report quotes accurately, I can tell you that for nothing.'

'Yes, heat of the moment. That might be it. Would that be why you also said, "How would this so-called journalist appreciate her whole life being ruined"?' She stared at him, letting the question linger in the air between them.

Callum Woods swallowed and folded his arms. 'I don't remember saying that.'

'You don't need to. It's here in black and white,' Ryan replied, waving the photocopied article in the air.

Woods stayed silent for a few moments. 'Listen, what's this all about? You've sent CID up here from some bloody Home Counties backwater to question me over a quote in a newspaper article from over a year ago?'

'Funny that you remember the date, but nothing else,' Ryan said. 'Is anything else springing to mind by any chance?'

It seemed to Wendy that Woods was trying to stare Ryan out. 'Why don't you just tell me what this is all about?' he said, eventually.

Wendy decided that now was the best time to chip in. 'Tanya Henderson was attacked on her front doorstep in front of her four-year-old daughter on Sunday evening. The attack was so severe that Tanya has been put on a specialist brain injury unit. She's been in an induced coma since she got there.'

Callum Woods's blinking increased in speed. 'Right. And?'

'And we're looking to speak to anyone who might have had a reason to want Tanya Henderson harmed. As I'm sure you can understand,' Wendy said.

'Are you serious? You must have a list as long as your arm, then. Have you seen the sort of stuff that woman writes? She ruins lives for a living. She's done it to hundreds of people, not just me.'

'Oh, so you've remembered who she is now?' Ryan interjected.

Wendy raised her hand slightly to placate Ryan. 'It's a matter of routine, Mr Woods. But where were you on Sunday evening?'

'Easy. At home, like I always am,' he said, sitting back and clearly relaxing a little. 'I'm usually pretty bloody knackered the day after a game. Besides which, we're not allowed late nights during the season, especially not before Monday morning training. And I'm a good little boy.' Woods threw a knowing glance at Ryan — one she intercepted and interpreted without any problem at all.

'Do you have an alibi?' Wendy asked.

'My missus and the kids. Although the kids were in bed by seven and the missus was asleep by eleven.'

Wendy nodded. If that could be corroborated, it would rule Woods out of any direct involvement. It wouldn't go too far towards proving his innocence entirely, though. There was still every possibility that someone else had done the dirty work for him. If Wendy had to be honest, this was the line of enquiry she was expecting to follow most closely. After all, famous people didn't tend to make the best criminals.

'Do you have a garage or shed at all?' Wendy asked.

'Yeah, both. There's a shed in the garden full of kids' toys and patio furniture and stuff, and a triple garage at the side.'

'Mind if we take a look?' Wendy asked.

Woods shook his head and sighed. 'Fine with me. The shed's probably a bit pointless, though, unless you're looking for a particular model of trike or sun lounger.'

Callum Woods led them through to his impressive garage and flicked on the light. It appeared to be heated, too.

'No cars in here?' Wendy asked.

'No, they're in the other building over there,' Woods replied, gesturing with his hands. 'It's got better security.'

Wendy nodded. 'Makes sense. Not got many tools in here, have you?'

Woods laughed. 'Well no. Unsurprisingly. I'm not exactly a DIY kind of guy. I have people come in to do all that stuff. I'm not exactly doing too badly, you know.'

Wendy could detect just a hint of arrogance in his voice as she tugged on various drawers and cupboard handles. One cupboard door seemed to have far less give in it than the others. In fact, it wouldn't budge at all.

'This one locked?' she asked, knowing full well that it wasn't as it didn't have a lock on it.

'Oh, nah it's just jammed. I think some of the wood's warped. We like to keep the heat on in here but the previous owners didn't, so some of the wood was a bit damp when we moved in.'

'Ah. The joy of garages,' Wendy said. 'Don't suppose you've got a crowbar handy, have you?' She watched carefully for his reaction.

'I dunno. Doubt it. I'll have a look,' he said, walking over to the other side of the large garage to look inside a drawer.

Ryan leaned in towards Wendy and whispered, 'Nice. What about the shed?'

'We can't do much about that. We can't force him to let us in there without a warrant.'

'We could get one.'

Wendy raised her eyebrows momentarily. 'Possible. Although we'd need something more to get it signed off. Public figure and all that.'

'Nope, nothing here,' Woods said, closing the drawer. 'Then again, I wouldn't know the difference between a crowbar and a power drill.'

Wendy smiled. Somehow she doubted that.

33

Before the morning briefing had even got going, Jack Culverhouse's pounding headache was made momentarily worse by the ringing of his desk phone. He was already two bodies short, with Wendy Knight and Ryan Mackenzie up in the East Midlands speaking to Callum Woods, and he didn't feel in any fit state to be getting further depressed by the team's lack of progress.

'Culverhouse,' he barked into the phone, his throat raw.

It was the desk sergeant. 'There's a woman here to see you about the Tanya Henderson case. A Chloe Robinson. She says you met her at the hospital yesterday.'

He vaguely remembered the name. A nurse, he thought.

'I'll be right down.'

He groaned something at Frank Vine about suspending the morning briefing, then made his way down the corridor before taking the three flights of stairs down to the front desk. He usually would've taken the lift, but this morning he knew he could do with having the blood flow to his brain. Not to mention the fact that the movement of the lift might make him liable to vomit.

He recognised the nurse immediately as soon as he got to the front desk and, after greeting her, he took her into a side room.

'How's Tanya doing?' he asked, assuming that she hadn't come down here to give him an update on her medical condition, but interested all the same.

'No news,' the nurse replied. 'She's stable, but there's not really anything new.'

'Good. Well, no news is good news.'

'Indeed.'

Culverhouse could sense there was something she wanted to tell him — after all, she'd come here for a reason — but at the same time she didn't seem to be saying all that much.

'So how can I help you?' he said, trying to be as diplomatic as possible. His head was pounding and he'd much rather have been at home asleep. 'I mean, I presume this isn't a social visit.'

'Oh. No. Well, you see, it's a bit weird. It's about yesterday, when Tanya was brought out of her coma.'

'What about it?' Culverhouse said, his patience running thin.

'Well, actually it's more about what happened just before she was sedated again. She seemed confused and she was saying all sorts of odd things. I didn't think much of it at the time, because it's fairly common for patients with brain injuries to come out with strange things, but it was only when I was reading the newspaper later in the evening that it started to make sense. She was mumbling, and it was difficult to hear what she was saying, but I definitely heard "crowbar" a few times.'

'She was attacked with a crowbar,' Culverhouse said.

'I know. That's what I mean. Yet earlier she said she couldn't recall anything about what happened. Then, when she got all agitated, she remembered the crowbar.'

Culverhouse knew this could be significant, but he wasn't sure how. 'Could there be a medical reason for that? For why she remembered it when she was agitated, but not when she was calm? Earlier, I mean.'

The nurse shrugged. 'I don't know. Not that I know of.'

'And did she say anything else?' he asked.

'Nothing relevant, I don't think,' she replied, clearly thinking back. 'She kept talking about the bright lights in the room, and I think she said "Pevensey Park" a few times.'

'Pevensey Park?' Culverhouse said. 'Where's that?'

'I don't know. And she said something about having to go to a meeting. "I have to go", she kept saying. Look, I wouldn't normally even bother reporting this because we get things like this all the time. Elderly women who suddenly become convinced they're twenty-one again. Just general delirium. It's pretty common. But the crowbar thing threw me. She's obviously got the memories there. We just need to find a way of getting them out of her.'

Culverhouse couldn't agree more. 'The only problem with that is that she's already reacted really badly to being brought out of her coma. I don't think the doctors will be in any great rush to try again, will they?'

'Well, no. I imagine they'll leave it a good few days. They'll want to see tangible improvements rather than just having her remain stable.'

Culverhouse nodded slowly. He had the distinct impression that Chloe Robinson was holding something back.

'And is there anything else?'

'How do you mean?' she replied, forcing a smile.

'Anything else on your mind? Something you might have seen, heard, thought of? I mean, you're with Tanya Henderson most of the time on the ward. Is there anything you've... observed?'

Chloe pushed her bottom lip out and slowly shook her head. 'Not that I can think of. To be honest, she's been unconscious most of the time and there was a police presence there when she was awake.'

'Except for those crucial two or three minutes,' he said, more frustrated at himself than anything. 'Here's a thought. The security cameras on the ward. Was there one near Tanya's bed?'

The nurse narrowed her eyes. 'Well yes, but I don't think there's any suggestion of anything untoward...'

'No, I know,' Culverhouse said. 'But do you think it

might have picked up Tanya's words? We might be able to go back and listen, see what she was saying.'

'Ah. No can do, I'm afraid. The cameras don't do sound.'

Culverhouse smiled and nodded, but inside he was fuming. What exactly had been the point in Chloe Robinson's visit, other than to point out another missed chance to gather some crucial evidence?

'Right. Well, give me a call if you think of anything else. Anything useful,' he added, not very subtly, as he escorted the nurse from the room.

He watched as she left through the automatic doors at the front of the building, cursing silently to himself. He knew it was going to be one of those days.

34

Culverhouse hated texting, but right now he didn't particularly want to speak to anyone. He selected Wendy's contact details from his phonebook and typed out the message.

How long?

She'd know what he meant. He really couldn't be bothered to type any more.

He took the flights of stairs a little more slowly on the way up, feeling his legs ache with every step as the sun dazzled him through the floor-to-ceiling glass windows on each level of the staircase. The grass outside looked so green and inviting, and he wished he could be out there, sitting on it.

Rounding the corner of the landing on the next floor, he continued his steps up just as his phone buzzed in his pocket.

Taking it out, he looked at the screen.

Not long. On way back. Hour maybe?

There you go, he thought. Much easier than making a phone call.

Of course, he wasn't entirely sure what he was going to have them do when they got back; this whole investigation seemed to be on the go-slow. For as long as Tanya was unconscious, there was very little they could do. There was no evidence as to what she had been working on at the time she was attacked, there were no witnesses, no murder weapon had been found, and there were either no suspects or hundreds of the fuckers depending on your outlook. Whichever way you looked at it, it wasn't great.

Jack knew the Chief Constable wouldn't be happy. Charles Hawes was generally a very forgiving man as far as Jack Culverhouse was concerned, but even he had his limits. He was slowly but surely running out of lives, and with Hawes approaching retirement age, he knew he wouldn't have an ally sitting in the main seat for much longer.

Regardless, he knew he had to keep him up to speed and now was as good a time as any. At least it *looked* like things were happening. Wendy and Ryan were up in the East Midlands speaking to Callum Woods, Debbie Weston was still going through Tanya's financial and phone records with a fine-tooth comb — even though they already knew there was absolutely nothing there — and after the case had been covered in the local papers, they'd received a handful of calls from the public.

If it were any other investigation, progress wouldn't be looking too bad at all, but Jack knew this was all a front. It was a case of looking busy, knowing damn well that Tanya Henderson's security consciousness could have been her own downfall. And until she came round again — *if* she came round again — there was very little they could do to help her.

He knocked on the door of Charles Hawes's office and waited for a couple of seconds. There was no answer, so he knocked again.

'Come in,' came the familiar voice from the other side. So he did.

There were many faces Jack wouldn't have been particularly keen to see that morning, but Martin Cummings's was right up there. The county's Police and Crime Commissioner was the worst conceivable career politician, elected as the first PCC for the county in the initial set of elections. Jack thought it had been a stupid idea from the start, having an elected politician effectively in charge of the local police forces of Britain, but it had been the flagship policy of the government of the day and there wasn't a whole lot he could do about it.

It would be fair to say, too, that Martin Cummings wasn't Jack Culverhouse's biggest fan. Cummings was very much a reformer, keen on merging police resources and centralising everything up at Milton House, the county's police headquarters. It was only the high success rate of Mildenheath CID's recent investigations and Charles Hawes's continued insistence that ensured their unit still existed. Without the continued success or the dogged determination of the Chief Constable, the whole team would've been subsumed into Milton House by now, doubtless run by DCI Malcolm Pope — or *Malcolm Fucking Pope* as he was known to Jack.

It felt like they were hanging on by a thread, and the weight attached to it was increasing all the time.

'Ah, Jack. Perfect timing. I was just trying to update the Commissioner about the progress on the Tanya Henderson case.'

Culverhouse didn't say anything; he just stared at Cummings.

'Are we any closer to finding out what happened?' Cummings asked.

'Getting closer all the time,' Culverhouse replied. 'All the time.'

Cummings nodded. 'Good,' he said, elongating the word. 'So what can we tell the press? I've been fending off their calls all day. They're pretty keen on this. They're all over it, seeing as she's one of their own. They won't let it go. They want an update.'

'I'm sure they do. And when we've got something we can help them with, or something they can help us with, I'll let them know.'

'By which you mean you're no closer to having a suspect or any sort of usable evidence, I suppose?'

Culverhouse forced a smile. 'Getting closer all the time.'

'Right. Only *time* is the operative word here, isn't it? From what I've been told, I understand there's a decent chance Tanya Henderson might not pull through this. In which case we're looking at a murder case.'

'Yes, I'm well aware of that. But I'm not quite sure what you've been told, because the facts are that she's currently in a stable condition.' Culverhouse didn't want to mention the fact that there was also a strong chance Tanya Henderson's attacker might be trying to get to her again. Some things were best left unsaid, especially around the Police and Crime Commissioner.

Martin Cummings was quiet for a few moments. 'Do you need some help, Jack?' he said, almost sounding sincere.

'Help?'

'With the investigation, I mean. If it's a case of manpower, I can have some people sent down. DCI Pope's very keen to get involved.'

Jack clenched his teeth. He could smell the thinly-veiled threat a mile off. 'Yeah, I bet he is.'

'Well, the offer's there if you need it,' Cummings said, smiling as he rose from his chair and extended his hand for him to shake. Jack stared at it for a couple of moments before acquiescing. 'Just give me a call, alright? That's what we've got resources for.'

Resources, Culverhouse thought. Great way to refer to dedicated serving police officers. He said nothing, just watched Cummings leave.

'He's got a point, Jack,' the Chief Constable said from behind him. 'Seriously. Do you need anything?'

Culverhouse let out a deep breath.

'Yeah. Yeah, I do. Couple of paracetamol would be great.'

Culverhouse quietly turned the brass key, locking the door to the stationery store from the inside. He used his hands to feel behind him, running his fingers along the wooden shelving and down, trying to find a place to sit.

He finally settled between two large boxes containing reams of A4 paper, leaning back against a packet of display-board-sized coloured card. It was dark, quiet, and smelled of fresh paper. It was a comforting scent, and one that he filled his nostrils with as he took deep, calming breaths. In through his nose, out through his mouth. In through his nose, out through his mouth.

He leaned his head back against the vertical shelf divider, feeling it rest in the indentation in the rear-middle of his skull. It wasn't especially comfortable, but it was more than fine.

The cold of the floor tiles started to seep through his

trousers, cooling his buttocks. He raised his knees, brought his feet towards him and rested his arms on his knees.

There was a chink of light coming through under the door, and after looking at it for a few seconds, willing it to go away, he slid one of the boxes of printer paper over with his foot, covering the gap.

Now it was completely black. It was also completely silent.

Closing his eyes, he allowed his mind to rest and inevitably start wandering. He could feel his eyelids flickering, his overactive brain desperately firing pulses to every part of his body as if he'd just downed five double espressos. His head felt as though someone had placed a wet battery on either temple, sending a small charge of electricity straight through his skull.

He'd felt like this once or twice before. It wasn't often that things got too much for him, but when they did, he knew he had to deal with it in the right way.

The last time this happened had been in the aftermath of the Ripper killings, during which a local psychopath had decided to emulate the murders of the infamous Jack the Ripper right here in Mildenheath. It was a case that had almost ended his career, with national and even international media attention. Far too many lives were lost, including that of PC Luke Baxter, for whom he'd had high hopes. That was, until he'd watched him take a bullet for him before practically dying in his arms.

It was around the time of the Ripper killings that

Helen had first returned, swanning back into his life as if nothing had happened. Except things *had* happened. Too many things had happened. Seeing her again had had a marked impact on Jack. It had brought it all back, all that pain and misery that he was just about starting to leave behind.

The pressure of the Ripper case had certainly taken its toll on him, and he'd barely had time to catch his breath before he was thrown straight back into it. Not only had Helen disappeared off again, still on bad terms with him, but there had been another huge case to deal with as well.

In hindsight, it shouldn't have been a huge case. A sex offender had been brutally tortured and killed in his own home. It should have been a straightforward murder case, but nothing was straightforward in Jack Culverhouse's mind at that time. His off-kilter mental state had meant that a second murder — of another sex offender — had been committed before they'd got close to fully investigating the first. And when Jack had foolishly suggested that the investigation wasn't a priority because the killer was cleaning up the filth for them, it was fair to say that those in authority didn't agree with him. His ensuing suspension from the investigation had almost destroyed him.

But Jack Culverhouse was a fighter. And, yet again, he'd been there to save the day. He couldn't not be. He knew that as soon as there came a time when he wasn't, it would all be over, and that wasn't a possibility he was willing to entertain.

He wasn't sure if he'd nodded off, but he was jolted into full consciousness by his mobile phone vibrating in his pocket. He took it out and looked at it, the bright screen making him squint as he struggled to read the name of Antonio García on the screen.

'Yeah?' he said, in a hoarse whisper as he answered the call.

'Jack? Have I caught you asleep?' Antonio said, sounding more concerned than joking.

'Oh. No. I'm just in a meeting, so I have to talk quietly.'

'Ah, I see. Well I won't keep you long, but I needed to call you to give you an update.'

Culverhouse swallowed hard. 'Go on.'

'Leandro called me. He and his colleague have been watching quite closely, trying to get some more information for you, like you asked. Earlier today, while they were watching, they were approached by two men from the *Guardia Civil* who had also been keeping an eye on the property. It turns out they had been tipped off that this woman and the girl were unregistered immigrants. Since 2007, every person living in Spain for more than three months has to register with the *Oficina de Extranjeros*. These two people had not registered. The property was listed as uninhabited, you see.'

Culverhouse could feel his heart racing. 'Get to the point, Antonio.'

'Alright, alright. Listen, Jack. They took them in for questioning, the woman and the girl. And they got to the bottom of who they are. It turns out they're Swedish.'

He paused for a moment. 'Swedish?'

'Yes. I'm sorry, Jack, but the girl isn't Emily.'

36

Wendy quite often got annoyed by Jack Culverhouse's attitude, and today was no different.

She could put up with him being obnoxious and offensive — she'd learnt to just blank that out in her mind — but she couldn't deal with him going AWOL for hours on end, effectively leaving her to lead the investigation in his place.

She wasn't quite sure how she'd got to that point, either. He was the DCI, he was in charge. She wasn't even the most experienced DS on the team — Steve Wing and Frank Vine had worked on the major crimes unit for years before she'd joined. Even Debbie Weston, although she was only a DC, had years of service on her. But at the same time she knew there was no way that Steve or Frank would ever step up to the mark. Even if the job was going, they wouldn't go for it. They were perfectly happy being sergeants, waiting out their remaining years before they could retire. That left Wendy as the one who had to step up when Culverhouse couldn't.

The last thing she knew, he'd got a phone call and had gone downstairs, but that was almost two hours ago, and he wasn't answering his mobile. In the meantime, there were things that needed to be done. Decisions that needed to be made. Decisions that Culverhouse would no doubt disagree with, and even if he *did* agree with them, he'd disagree with her making them in his absence. She couldn't win.

She decided that the best thing to do was some chasing up — that would give Culverhouse an extra half an hour to return. But after that, she'd have to start taking control.

Picking up her mobile, she scrolled through her contacts list to Xavier Moreno's name and tapped *Dial*. She knew that even if Xav had no further information, he'd still be friendly about it.

'Hi Wendy,' he said, when he finally answered. 'How are you?'

'Yeah, I'm good. Listen, I was just wondering if you had any luck getting a closer look at Tanya Henderson's machine. I spoke to Milton House yesterday morning and requested you personally. I don't know if it did any good.'

'My boss did mention something about an approach, but he didn't seem to take it too seriously. I think he wants to keep me on the team here, to be honest. Thing is, with the budget cuts they tend not to replace civilian staff who leave unless they're absolutely vital. And I'm probably not.'

'Ah. Well maybe I'll have another word with them then. Thing is, we're pretty stuck at this end. Tanya Henderson was brought out of her coma yesterday, but she ended up getting really agitated and confused so they upped the dosage again. The doctors were worried she was going to cause herself harm, or that her brain would start to swell again.'

'That doesn't sound good,' Xav said.

'No, tell me about it. But we know there's stuff on that machine. That's where she kept all of her work documents and everything. If we can just get into that, we'd be home and dry. We'd be able to find her attacker within hours.'

From the other end of the phone, Wendy heard him sigh heavily.

'It's really not that easy, Wendy.'

'I know it isn't. But there's the slightest possibility, right? You need to help me, Xav. I'm at my wits' end.'

Xav was silent for a few moments. 'Are you in tonight?'

Wendy looked at her watch. 'Yeah, I'll be home around half six. Why?'

'I'll pop over at eight,' he said.

She beamed a big smile, somehow hoping he might be able to see it at the other end of the line. 'Thanks, Xav. You're a star.'

The sound of Wendy putting the phone down coincided with the clatter of the door to the incident room opening, followed by Jack Culverhouse marching through to get to his office. He didn't say a word, but everyone could quite clearly see that it would be best not to try and speak to him.

Wendy looked down at her list of other people she needed to chase, wondering how much time that might take up.

37

It's often said that in times of stress and anxiety, man reverts to type, and that was certainly the case with Jack as he made his way back to the incident room. Without saying a word, he secreted himself in his office, locking the door behind him and lowering the blinds.

Although he had an office of his own (or, rather, a stud-wall partition with some windows in it) he rarely used it, except for times when he really did not want to be disturbed or had to speak to someone in private. The rest of the time he preferred to be out there on the floor, keeping up to speed with what was going on. To him, offices meant managers, paperwork and red tape; they didn't mean policing.

Sitting down at his desk, he logged on to his computer, the bubble in the corner of the screen telling him he had twenty-three new emails. Thankfully, the bubble disappeared after a few seconds.

He opened up his web browser, went to Google and typed in *Pevensey Park*. The ancient internet connection took an age to load the results, but when it did he was met with a list of pages, most of which seemed to refer to Pevensey Bay, in East Sussex. He searched again, this time with the words in speech marks. That should give him a list of exact matches.

The results list showed him some pages regarding property prices in a couple of streets called Pevensey Park Road, and then a link to the website for a park in the state of Victoria, Australia. Although it advertised itself as 'the perfect place for kids to play and enjoy activities', it looked more like a graveyard than a play park. Besides which, it was situated on the other side of the world. What possible connection could Tanya Henderson have to it? The web page told Jack nothing else; it just simply linked to a list of other similarly depressing-looking parks in the area.

Going back to the Google results page, he kept scrolling down. It was all about property prices. The second page had nothing either, but he skipped on to the third page just to be sure. There, nestled at the bottom of the page, was a link to the Mildenheath History Society's website.

Jack's heart skipped a beat. This had to be the connection. He clicked the link.

The page seemed to take forever to load, but when it did he was met with a rather garish-looking black background laden with dense white text and some very 1990s-style animated GIFs. He mused to himself that the

Mildenheath History Society must have used the same web designer as county CID did for their intranet.

In the centre of the screen was an old black and white photograph of a vast expanse of field, a couple of trees dotted about and some children sitting on a picnic blanket, enjoying the summer sun. The caption read *Local youths enjoying themselves, circa 1937.*

He skim-read the article, trying to pick up the salient points as quickly as possible before going back and reading the whole thing through again. There was one paragraph that caught his eye.

Following the outbreak of the Second World War, the Mildenheath area was designated as a prime location for evacuees from London. With the increase in local population, the growing urbanisation of the town and the very real threat of bomb attacks or invasion, the district council sped through long-talked-about plans to build a hospital on the outskirts of Mildenheath. A number of locations were mooted, but the council quickly settled on Pevensey Park. New play areas were built nearby, on Rothesay Street and McKittrick Drive.

He sat back in his chair. Pevensey Park used to be located on the site where Mildenheath General Hospital now stood. The hospital in which Tanya Henderson was currently lying in an induced coma. But, try as he might, he couldn't quite see a connection. At least, the only one he *could* see was incredibly disappointing.

As a journalist living locally, it was entirely possible that Tanya Henderson could have been more than aware of the history of the town. After all, this seemed to be publicly-available knowledge. It would be there in the back of her mind while she was in the hospital, and in her anxious, delirious state she'd simply mumbled the thoughts of her subconscious mind, the same way sleepwalkers sometimes do. Jack was no medical expert, but it all seemed to make perfect sense.

He scrolled back up the top of the website and clicked on the *Contact* button. The page that loaded had a contact form on it, as well as a phone number for the Society's secretary, Colin Walsh. He picked up his mobile and called the number on the page. It rang a few times before going through to voicemail, giving him the phone network's standard anonymous greeting.

He paused for a couple of moments, then logged onto the Police National Computer system and loaded up the Drivers database. This particular database was kept up to date by the Driver and Vehicle Licensing Agency every morning, and it contained the names and details of everyone in the country who either held a driving licence or were banned from driving. He typed in Colin Walsh's name and narrowed the search down to the local area. A few seconds later, he had an address.

Walking over to the door to the incident room, he

unlocked it, pushing it open just enough to get his head through the gap.

'Mackenzie, in here.'

DC Ryan Mackenzie did as she was told, quickly walking into Culverhouse's office and closing the door behind her.

'You're young,' Culverhouse said. 'What's that thing you can do where you find out who owns a website?'

Ryan cocked her head slightly. 'What, you mean a WHOIS lookup?'

'Yeah, one of them. Find out who owns this site, will you?'

Ryan stopped in her tracks. 'I think that's probably best done by the IT guys,' she said. 'I don't really want to risk—'

'Just do it, alright? I can't be waiting four days for those fuckers to get back to me when you can do it in thirty seconds.'

Ryan could see by the look on Culverhouse's face that she didn't have much of a choice. 'I'll do it on my iPhone,' she said eventually. 'It's not a work one, so it shouldn't flag up on the network.'

Culverhouse watched as she navigated to the right website on her phone, pleased that he'd at least managed to put one chink in her goody-two-shoes armour.

'Right. According to the registration details it's in the name of Mildenheath History Society, number 20 Hennessy Street.'

Culverhouse looked down at his notepad, on which he'd written the address from the PNC.

'Perfect.'

Hennessy Street was probably only a five or ten minute walk from the office, but he decided to drive anyway.

He parked up on the pavement outside number 20 and killed the engine. Like many of the houses at this end of Mildenheath, it was a tall Victorian terraced building, with a small courtyard front garden.

He opened the gate and walked up to the door, pressing his finger down on the doorbell for a good few seconds.

He could see a dark figure approaching the door, and he waited as the occupant undid all manner of chains and locks. When the door finally opened, he was met by a man he could only presume to be the secretary of the Mildenheath History Society.

'Colin Walsh?'

'Yeah,' the man said, looking slightly confused.

Culverhouse flashed his warrant badge. 'DCI Jack Culverhouse, Mildenheath CID. Alright if I pop in for a second?' he said, having already barged his way past Colin Walsh.

'Uh, yeah, okay. What's it... Uh, do you want a cup of tea or something?'

'No thanks,' Culverhouse said, from the living room. 'I won't be staying long. I did try to call you, but your number went straight through to answerphone.'

'Oh right. Yes. It's upstairs charging,' Colin replied, finally catching up with him in the living room. 'Probably on silent. Battery doesn't last five minutes on them these days.'

'No problem. Thought I'd better pop over instead. Does the name Tanya Henderson ring any bells?' he said, catching the homeowner off-guard, watching his face for any flicker of recognition.

'No... I can't say it does. Should it?'

'That's what I'm here to find out. Do you keep records of the members of your history society?'

Colin Walsh looked momentarily confused. 'Well, yes. They're all stored on the computer.'

'Are they accessible now?'

'Yes... Yes, they are. I'd have to take a look, though. We've recently moved over onto a new system, you see. It allows people to sign up using a web link, then it automatically puts them into the database and sends out a welcome email to them with all of the information. Means I don't have to do anything at this end. So if she's a member, I probably wouldn't know about it without actually looking at the list.'

Culverhouse forced a fake smile. 'So, can we look at it then?'

'Yes, of course,' Colin said, sitting down at the computer, which was situated just inside the dining room section of his open-plan lounge-diner. 'Here we are. Members' Database. You'll have to give it a minute. It takes a little while to load.'

Culverhouse could feel his patience wearing thin. He gritted his teeth.

'Ah yes. Right. What did you say her name was? Tracey what?'

'Henderson,' Culverhouse said. 'Tanya Henderson.'

'Righto,' Colin replied, typing more slowly than Culverhouse had ever seen anyone type in his life. 'Is that with an I or with a Y?'

'With a Y,' Culverhouse replied, desperate to lean over and type it in himself.

'Righto. Hen...der...son. Got it. Ah yes. She is a member. Manor Way, does that sound about right?'

'It sounds very right,' Culverhouse said. 'How long's she been a member for?'

'Hmmmm... Let me see... Ah. Yes. She joined three weeks ago, apparently. Why, has she done something wrong?' Colin said, turning round in his chair to face Culverhouse.

Culverhouse sighed. 'That's exactly what I'm trying to find out.'

38

The incident room seemed to be buzzing when Culver-house got back. There was a frisson in the air, which was noticeable from the moment he walked in through the door.

'Guv, you're never going to guess what,' Debbie Weston said, holding up a sheet of A4 paper. 'We've been looking into Callum Woods a bit further. Phone records, property details, things like that. We went back a fair way, and we—'

'Sorry, what?' Culverhouse said, interrupting her, his face like thunder. 'Where did you get clearance for that?'

'From the Chief Constable,' Debbie replied.

'You went straight to him?'

'Well, no, I didn't,' she replied, not saying any more.

'So who did?' Culverhouse's voice was calm and quiet, which made it even more unnerving than if he'd been shouting at the top of his lungs.

Wendy took a deep breath. 'I did.'

The DCI's head snapped round in her direction. 'And why didn't you go through me?'

'I tried, but I couldn't find you. Time was of the essence, especially seeing as Woods knew we were looking at him after our visit. We couldn't risk him trying to cover anything up or hide anything.'

'You're supposed to go through me,' was all Culverhouse said.

'And I would have done, but you weren't here.' Wendy's tone was firm, insinuating that she wasn't going to take any shit from him over this.

Fortunately, he backed down.

'And what did you find?' he asked Debbie.

'Well, get this. His credit card statement showed a payment to a company called Dunlop, Briggs and Paver. They're a firm of solicitors based just outside town. That got me thinking, why was he using a firm of solicitors from Mildenheath when he lives nowhere near here? They wouldn't tell me anything on the phone without a specific warrant, but their website tells me they're property planning and conveyancing specialists. A bit of digging showed that Callum Woods recently applied for an extension on his house, and logic says that Dunlop, Briggs and Paver were the solicitors he used for the application. The dates seem to match up. But there's more. I pulled up the deeds on his property. The company he used to build the house in the first place was a company called Avalon Construction. They're local, too, and work closely with Dunlop,

Briggs and Paver, apparently — they recommend their legal services for new builds.'

'Right, so he used a company based around here to have his house built and extended. So what?'

'So you're going to love the next bit. I looked up Avalon Construction's details at Companies House. One of its directors is a Mr Gary McCann.'

Culverhouse was silent for a couple of seconds. 'You're having a fucking laugh,' he said, eventually.

'Nope. He owns seven percent of the shares, apparently.'

Culverhouse tried to get his head around what this meant. Callum Woods, a professional footballer who claimed to have no links with the Mildenheath area, and who said he'd never even heard of the place, used both a building company and a firm of solicitors from there, miles away from his home. Not only that, but one of the shareholders of the building company was one of the area's biggest crooks — something Culverhouse had never been able to prove, though not for want of trying. There was now a link, not only between Callum Woods and Mildenheath — the town in which Tanya Henderson, the woman who'd nearly ruined his career, lived — but an admittedly more tenuous one between Callum Woods and Gary McCann too.

'That's nothing we can question him about, though, is it?' Culverhouse said. 'I mean, we're not even out of the realms of coincidence yet. McCann has shares in hundreds of companies, and Avalon Construction are a big name. It's hardly inconceivable that they'd build Callum Woods's house. They do projects all over the country, from what I've heard.'

'Yeah, but add that onto Callum Woods's bad boy image and the fact that Gary McCann's one of the dodgiest buggers in the country, and what are we looking at?' Debbie said.

'That's the wording you're going to give to the CPS, is it?' Culverhouse replied. 'Yeah, I can see them running with that. Listen, it's good. It's a great start. But we need to dig deeper. We need to find out more. But I think we'd be better off doing that tomorrow.'

'It's alright. I applied for overtime,' Debbie said.

Culverhouse opened his mouth to ask her who'd authorised that, but thought better of it. Without a twenty-four hour CID operation at Mildenheath, the occasional granting of overtime during a busy case was all they could hope for.

The only alternative was to hand overnight duties to a team at Milton House, and that wasn't a possibility he was willing to entertain.

39

The doorbell rang shortly before eight o'clock, and Wendy enjoyed the sound of her heels clip-clopping across the wooden flooring in her hall as she made her way to the door.

She'd left work a little earlier than usual so she could come home and spend quite some time getting ready. With Xav having invited himself over again, she knew things were now at the stage where she'd have to make sure she didn't cock it up. From her own experience, and from what she'd seen, police officers — and CID ones in particular — had a wonderful ability of not being able to separate their work from their social lives.

Work inevitably got in the way of relationships and caused more harm than good. She'd seen it a hundred times over, and she certainly didn't want it happening to her. She'd already had her fair share of bad luck. This time, she was going to remain in control.

She smiled as she opened the door to reveal Xav, a little more casually dressed than he had been two nights previous, but still managing to look more than good.

'Come in,' she said. 'Glass of wine?'

'I'm driving,' he replied, stepping inside the door.

'Ah. Well you can just have one, can't you? A small one, I mean.'

'Nah, better not,' Xav said, raising his hand slightly. 'Don't want to risk it. Anyway, I can't stay long.'

'Oh.'

There was an awkward pause while the two of them stood in the hallway, staring at each other.

'You look nice,' he said, eventually.

'Thanks.'

'Off out somewhere?'

Wendy swallowed. 'Uh, yeah. Just out to meet some friends.'

'Cool.'

'Do you want to come in? Sit down for a minute?'

Xav smiled out of the corner of his mouth, then made his way through to the living room. When he got there, he sat down in the armchair, leaving Wendy hovering. Finally, she sat down on the arm of the sofa, cradling her wine glass.

'So. What's new? You said you might be able to do something with Tanya Henderson's laptop.'

Xav looked down at the floor. 'Listen, Wendy,' he said, fidgeting in his seat, 'that's kind of what I came to talk to you about, yes. But it's more than that.'

Wendy didn't like the sound of where this was going.

'How do you mean?'

'I just feel... Look, you didn't call me after the other night. No texts, nothing. Not until this afternoon, when you called up wanting more information from me. That doesn't make a guy feel good.'

No matter how much she knew he was right, Wendy still couldn't help feeling defensive. 'Xav, what do you want me to do? I'm in the middle of a big investigation. And you're the best damn IT guy we've got. Far better than any of the forensic IT people. They're only interested in ticking boxes and covering their arses. You're the best. Of course I'm going to come to you.'

'So, all that stuff the other night. Y'know, when we...'

'Are you trying to ask me if it meant anything?' Wendy said. 'Because yes, of course it did. You don't think I did it just to... Well...'

'Use me? Yeah, the thought had crossed my mind.'

Wendy didn't know what to say. In retrospect she could see exactly where he was coming from. Yes, she should've called, but then so should he. Neither of them had called each other, neither of them had texted each other. So why was the onus on her?

'Hang on a sec,' she said. 'You can't have it both ways, Xav. You asked me to put in a good word at Milton House for you. You wanted me to help you get into forensic IT. But I'm not sitting here accusing you of using me, am I?'

Xav made a derisive noise as he shook his head. 'I'm not accusing you of anything, Wendy. I'm just saying that I don't want all this to be based on a quick fuck whenever you need help with a case. Don't get me wrong, I enjoyed the other night, of course I did, but it just makes me feel cheap.'

Standing up, Wendy went over to him, sitting on the arm of his chair. 'Xav, I'd be coming to you for help regardless, because you're the best there is. But yes, I find you attractive. And yes, I want to spend more social time with you. And, yes, I've been a complete dick and got myself so tied up in this case that I didn't call or text. I should've done. But you know as well as any what we're like when we get onto a case. It takes over. There's not a whole lot we can do.'

'What, and you don't even have time to send a text? Or make a quick phone call on your way home?'

'You didn't text me either, Xav. Anyway, it's not as easy as that. Sometimes I'm in meetings all day, or out interviewing witnesses. Sometimes I get home at stupid o'clock and just head straight to bed. It'll be better once this case is over, I promise.'

'And then what?' Xav replied, getting heated. 'Then you move on to the next case. Then the next case. Then the next case. This isn't something that ends. Not until you retire or leave the job, anyway.'

'That's not true,' she said, putting her hand on his shoulder. 'Look, let me prove it to you. Tonight's clearly a bit of a washout now, but how are you fixed for tomorrow night? I'll book us a nice table somewhere, alright?'

Xav nodded.

Wendy smiled. 'Alessandro's, eight o'clock. You have my word.'

40

The rest of the team had finally shuffled off home one-by-one, and Culverhouse eventually found himself doing the same.

When he got back to his place he glanced at the clock on the mantelpiece. Ten to midnight. Then he looked over at the drinks cabinet and the decanter of whisky, glowing golden in the half light. No. Not tonight, he told himself.

Instead he went into the kitchen and poured himself a glass of water, drinking half of it before his mobile phone started ringing on the coffee table, where he'd left it a moment earlier. He walked through and answered it, not recognising the number on the screen.

'Culverhouse.'

'Ah, Detective Chief Inspector. Sorry to call so late. It's Colin Walsh here, from the Mildenheath History Society. You came over to my house earlier, about the Henderson woman.'

'Yes. Hi. What can I do for you?' Culverhouse replied, walking back into the kitchen.

'I've been thinking about a couple of things you said. It didn't quite make sense at the time, but now I think it does. You see, after you left I called Alan Carnegie, who's our chief historian. He does a lot of local talks and things. Anyway, he mentioned that this Henderson woman had been in touch with him as well. Something to do with a local history group on Facebook. I don't know, I don't use it. But he recognised her name immediately when I told him about it. Said she'd been asking him questions about Pevensey Park.'

Culverhouse's heart skipped. 'What did he say?'

'Oh, she just wanted to find out about the history, and about the terms of sale when the council sold the land to build the hospital. But that's the funny thing, isn't it? It's the hospital she's in at the moment. She never really showed an interest in any other areas of local history other than Pevensey Park, apparently. Which is odd considering the fact that it was just a park, really. There wasn't a whole lot Alan could tell her.'

Culverhouse scrunched his eyes closed and scratched his head. 'Mr Walsh, is it alright if I call you in the morning? I think there's more we need to discuss, but it's late. I need a clear head.'

'Oh. Right. Yes, of course,' Colin said.

'Actually, can you give me a contact number for Alan Carnegie too? I'll need to give him a ring. Best if I speak with him directly.'

Colin Walsh reeled off a phone number, which Culverhouse wrote down on his kitchen notepad before thanking him and hanging up.

At the end of a long, stressful day, he was struggling to connect the dots and work out the significance of what this all meant, but he had the distinct feeling that they were starting to get somewhere — that this might just provide the loose thread that could unravel the whole mystery.

Thinking briefly of the whisky decanter again, he headed off to bed.

41

The next morning, Culverhouse phoned ahead to Alan Carnegie, agreeing to meet him at a coffee shop in the centre of Mildenheath. He was fine with that, as in his experience people tended to talk more openly and freely on neutral ground. In their own home they were far more guarded and tended to feel as though they were in control of the situation, whereas in a police station they tended to go into lockdown mode and say nothing of very much interest until the law got heavy and they had to either arrest or caution them — something they obviously couldn't do with witnesses.

It was fair to say that a large percentage of the local population weren't particularly keen on speaking to the police. Mildenheath had a bit of a reputation locally as being a town that had a high crime rate — something which was artificially skewed by its popularity as a drinking town on Friday and Saturday nights. The fact that a large amount of the anti-social behaviour was caused by people from outside of the town, or by people who otherwise wouldn't say boo to a goose, didn't change a thing. The police presence in Mildenheath was higher than in most towns, and that had the unfortunate effect of causing resentment amongst certain sections of the community.

Culverhouse was pleased to see Alan Carnegie — or the man he assumed to be Alan Carnegie — sitting at a seat near the window, nursing a latte. If he had to play Spot The Local Historian, this would be the first person he'd pick.

'Alan?' he asked, extending his hand. 'Jack Culverhouse. You alright for a drink?'

Alan Carnegie indicated that he was fine, and Culverhouse went and got himself a straight black coffee. Fortunately, the barista didn't ask him what type of coffee he wanted. As far as Jack Culverhouse was concerned, there was black coffee and white coffee, and even that was pushing it.

'I understand Tanya Henderson got in touch with you about something to do with local history,' he said, sitting back down. In his experience, it was always best to leave it to the witness to volunteer as much information as they wanted to — regardless of what you already knew.

'Yes,' replied Carnegie, smiling. 'She wanted to know about Pevensey Park, that's the area of land the hospital now sits on. It used to be a large public area. This is before the war, I'm talking about.'

'Surely it's a bit of an odd thing to ask about, isn't it? A park that hasn't existed for seventy-odd years. What sort of things was she asking?'

He stared into the distance for a moment. 'I find it difficult to remember exactly. I didn't think much of it, to be honest. But I do recall her asking about the terms of acquisition, when the land was acquired for the hospital. She wanted to know about leases, who now owned the land, what the terms were at the time with regards to reversion of rights. All that sort of stuff.'

Try as he might, Culverhouse couldn't see why she'd want to know any of this information. It was decades in the past, and anyone involved in the sale of Pevensey Park would likely be long dead. 'And what did you tell her?' he asked.

'There wasn't a whole lot I could tell her. I did a bit of research for her and we found out that the land was on a long-term lease for the hospital, and that the hospital trust bought a stake in it a few years back. There's nothing wrong with that, though. It happens quite a lot. Hospital trusts exist to ensure the future of the hospital, and to make sure they'll be in a secure financial position to offer the best possible care to patients. As I understand it.'

'But none of this makes any sense. Did she tell you what she was investigating?' Culverhouse asked.

'Nope. To be honest, I didn't ask. She just seemed interested.'

Culverhouse realised that the vast majority of people probably weren't interested in the history of the local area, and that Alan Carnegie had probably been only too happy to talk to her about it once she'd asked — much like how he seemed happy to talk to Culverhouse now. 'She is an investigative journalist, Mr Carnegie. She looks into allegations of corruption or wrongdoing, and writes articles exposing crooks. It's all very current stuff, though. She's hardly likely to be writing about the sale of some council land more than seven decades ago.'

'Ah, no, but the story doesn't end there,' Alan Carnegie said, leaning forward conspiratorially. He was definitely enjoying this. 'You see, being involved with the Mildenheath History Society does have its advantages. We have a member who works for the council, in their planning and development department. What if I were to tell you that there were plans afoot to merge Mildenheath Hospital's services into other county hospitals and clinics, sell the land and turn it into a huge housing development?'

'Well, I wouldn't be particularly surprised, but surely these things need public planning, consultation, all of that, don't they?'

'Yes, you'd think so, wouldn't you? And I've no doubt there will be a public consultation. All that means, though, is that they'll tell the public what they've already decided to do. These things are all done behind closed doors, Inspector. The decisions are made long before the possibility is even mentioned to the public. It's all about money and kickbacks.' He took a sip of his latte, shaking his head. 'You mark my words: if they're talking about the possibility of doing this, you can bet your bottom dollar the deal's already done.'

42

Culverhouse wasted no time in heading over to the council's offices. He'd tried to phone ahead to Alan Carnegie's contact, but he'd had no luck getting through. As he parked his car and went to get out, however, his phone rang.

'DCI Culverhouse? It's George Stretton here. I just got your message. Sorry, I couldn't answer my phone when you called as I'm at work.'

'Good. Because I'm sitting outside in the car park. Can you come out?'

'Oh. Well, I don't know. I mean, I'm technically on a break, but... What's this all about?'

'I'm investigating a very serious crime, and I think you might be able to help me with some information. Don't worry, you're not in trouble. But I can promise you it'll be made a whole lot easier if you come out and speak to me here.'

George Stretton suddenly sounded very nervous. 'How do you mean? Why can't you come in?'

'I can do, but then I'd have to ask for you by name at the front desk. There'd be a record of me visiting and speaking to you. So, you can either come out here and give me the information I need informally, off the record, or I can come in and get it from you in there, on the record and with your employer's knowledge. I'm happy either way, to be honest.'

Culverhouse could hear George Stretton swallowing at the other end of the phone. 'What's this all about?' he asked again. 'What makes you think I know anything that could help you? Or that I'd want to tell you?'

'One, I'll tell you what it's all about when you come out here. Two, we have a mutual friend who already told me what you know, but I need to hear it from you directly. Three, it's either that or a woman could die. You're going to have something on your conscience by the end of the day, whether it be blowing the whistle or letting an innocent woman be killed. Your choice, George.'

Culverhouse hung up the phone and waited.

Just over a minute later, the automatic doors at the entrance to the council building slid open and an ineffectual-looking man in his late fifties stepped out, glancing around. Culverhouse flashed his headlights, watching as the man paused for a moment before walking over. When he got to the car, George Stretton opened the passenger-side door and got in.

'Right,' said Culverhouse, not wasting any time on pleasantries, 'I'm going to cut straight to the chase. I need you to do something for me, George. I need you to tell me all about the plans for knocking down Mildenheath General Hospital and turning it into a housing estate, and I need you to tell me now.'

George Stretton seemed nervous, but relaxed. 'Inspector, you know as well as I do that all information is confidential...'

'Because otherwise,' Culverhouse continued, as if Stretton hadn't said anything at all, 'I'm going to go in that building right now and I'm going to speak to your boss. And I'm going to tell him everything that I already know, and I'm going to tell him it came from you. Either that, or you can tell me yourself. You can fill in the blanks for me, and no-one ever needs to know we spoke.'

George seemed to mull this over for a moment, but the logic was clear: it wasn't speaking to the police he was afraid of, rather that his bosses would find out he'd spoken to them. He swallowed before speaking.

'Look, there's nothing underhand about it,' he explained. 'These things happen all the time. The government is trying to make cuts in public expenditure, and the NHS is one of those areas. Hospitals cost a lot of money to maintain, and many of those services can easily be amalgamated into—'

'Cut the political shit, George. You're sitting in the

front seat of a fucking Volvo, not the panel of Question Time.'

'No, I know. And I need to tell you that nothing's definite yet, but there are some plans being put forward, yes.'

'Who's behind them?'

'Behind them?' George asked, seeming genuinely confused.

'Yes, behind the plans. Who first made the suggestion? Who put in the application? Who's lobbying for the hospital to be closed down and for the housing estate to be built?'

'Well, quite a few people. There's a consortium, of course, which—'

'Who's on it?'

'It's a combination of people,' replied a rather bewildered-looking George. 'Some are in favour, some against. At this stage it's just councillors and the hospital trust.'

Culverhouse tried not to show any reaction. He knew what this meant: if it was only a few councillors and the board of the hospital trust, there'd be a very good chance that a lot of decisions would already have been made before it was opened up to wider consultation. He knew from experience that this was the way local politics often worked: backroom deals done and dusted behind closed doors in the interest of profit, then the false illusion of democracy by putting it out to a public 'consultation', which they'd then ignore and steamroller their plans through anyway.

'Does the name Tanya Henderson mean anything to

you?' he asked George, keen to keep chopping and changing the subject slightly, trying to catch him off guard.

'What? No. Other than hearing that she was attacked. She's the reporter woman, isn't she?'

'Yes, she is. We think she might have been investigating something to do with the development of the hospital land. That's why we need to find out as much as we can. What are the plans?'

George shuffled in his seat slightly. 'The plan they're discussing at the moment is for forty-five houses. All fairly decent sized ones, nice gardens. They'd probably sell for half a million each, if you ask me. If not more. They're currently in the process of having private bids tabled by some local construction companies. But there's only one that'll get the job.'

'Who's that?' Culverhouse asked.

'The same one that always gets them. Avalon.'

'Avalon Construction?' Culverhouse asked, just to check he'd heard right. That was the company Gary McCann had a stake in. The same company that had built Callum Woods's house in the East Midlands.

'Yeah. They always get the jobs that the council's involved in. All the major ones, anyway. It's all a big fucking melting pot of backhanders and secret winks,' George said, starting to open up about the feelings he'd clearly been holding onto for quite some time. 'It's due to be announced to the public in the next couple of weeks, and then there'll be meetings and consultations, but they won't mean anything. The deal will be done by then.

Everything else is just a charade. Once they've decided they're going to do it, they'll do it. And nothing will stop them. Not with twenty-odd million quid at stake.'

Culverhouse suddenly realised exactly what Tanya Henderson had been trying to uncover, and why she had needed to uncover it so quickly. With Tanya lying in a coma in hospital, however, he knew the responsibility fell to one person: him.

43

Standing outside the large iron gates to Gary McCann's house, Culverhouse pressed the button on the intercom and waited for a response. As the speaker clicked and crackled, he spoke before the person on the other end could even get a word out.

'McCann, open up. We need to talk.'

'Sorry, who's this?' McCann replied, in a falsely jovial voice.

'You know exactly who it is. You're looking right at me,' Culverhouse said, raising his middle finger to the pinhole camera in the intercom unit.

A couple of seconds later, there was a loud click and the gates started whirring open. By the time Culverhouse had got to the end of the drive, the front door had also opened and the imposing figure of Gary McCann stood waiting for him on the doorstep.

'Detective Chief Inspector Culverhouse. It's been a

while. Coming to check that my tea and coffee making standards are still up to scratch?'

'Not for me, McCann. I wouldn't trust you to pour me a glass of water.'

'Let me know if you change your mind. I can promise you the milk's nowhere near as sour as you seem to be getting in your old age.'

'We all age at the same rate,' replied Culverhouse. 'Well, most of us do anyway. And how is the present Mrs McCann? She home from school yet?'

McCann smiled with one corner of his mouth. 'She's twelve years younger than me, Detective Chief Inspector. I'm quite sure you've got better jokes than that in your arsenal.'

'Oh, I've got plenty. Let me in and I'll tell you a few.'

McCann stared at him for a few moments before smiling and stepping aside, closing the door behind Culverhouse as he made his way through to the large living room.

'Come on then. Let's hear your best joke.'

Culverhouse sat down on a leather chesterfield, making his best display of flicking some dust from the armrest. 'I've got a belter for you, actually. A proper side-splitter. A councillor, a hospital trust board member and the dodgiest fucker in Mildenheath walk into a bar. You heard that one?'

McCann remained quiet and calm. 'I can't say I have. Tell me more.'

'I was rather hoping you could finish that one off for

me, actually. Because, try as I might, I can't find the fucking punchline for the life of me. In fact, some might say it's not very funny at all. Some might even call it a bit of a con.'

'I couldn't possibly say, Detective Chief Inspector. I don't know anything about cons,' he replied, as calm as ever.

'Of course not, McCann. Of course not. After all, you've never been *convicted* of one yet, have you?'

McCann smiled again. 'Feel free to keep trying, though. The apology letters look fantastic on the wall of my office.'

'Believe me, there's only one thing I intend to nail to the wall of your office. Two, in fact.'

'Careful, Detective Chief Inspector. That sounds almost like a threat.'

'There's a difference between a threat and a promise, McCann. Now. Tell me about Pevensey Park.'

McCann stretched, resting his arm on the back of the sofa and leaning back comfortably as he spoke. 'Somehow, I've a feeling you know more than I do. Or at least you think you do. But I'll give you the facts as they stand.'

'Changing the habit of a lifetime just for me,' Culverhouse said. 'I am honoured.'

McCann chose to ignore the remark. 'The hospital's going to close. There's not a whole lot we can do about that. Bigger decisions at higher levels. That'd already been decided before I got word of it. The only question is what's going to happen to the land. The local council are keen to see more housing in the area, what with the shortage and all, and they asked Avalon Construction to tender for the building work.'

'This is the same Avalon Construction that you own shares in, is that correct?'

'I have a small, non-controlling and non-voting stake in the company, yes. As I do in many companies.'

Culverhouse nodded. 'And what can you tell me about Callum Woods?'

'Who?'

'The footballer.'

McCann laughed. 'Not a whole lot. I don't follow football. What's that got to do with the hospital development?'

'That's what I'm trying to find out,' Culverhouse replied. 'Because Avalon Construction built his home in the East Midlands, a fair distance from here. They're also contracted to build his extension, and they recommended the firm of solicitors he's using to organise it.'

McCann shrugged. 'Avalon has a lot of customers all over the country, Detective Chief Inspector. We've probably built houses for hundreds of footballers.'

'Yes, but this one was the unfortunate target of an article by Tanya Henderson a year or so back, in which she almost singlehandedly ruined his career. The same Tanya Henderson who we believe was investigating the hospital development plans, and who was brutally attacked on her doorstep in front of her four-year-old daughter a few nights back.'

'Well, that all sounds very tenuous to me, I must say.'

'Oh, I'm sure it does. But that's the whole point, isn't it? A big wide circle of coincidences and events, but no direct cause and effect. That's the way all good corruption happens.'

Gary McCann leaned forward on the sofa, his elbows now resting on his knees. 'Let me tell you now, I know nothing of any footballer. I know nothing about Tanya Henderson. All I know is Avalon were asked to bid for the construction of houses on the hospital site. That's it.'

'Which is something you'd be very keen to see go through, isn't it?' Culverhouse said. 'I mean, that deal's worth more than twenty million quid. With your seven percent stake in the company, you're potentially looking at, what, well over a million. Possibly more. People have killed for a lot less.'

'I'm sure they have. And you and I both know I'm not exactly whiter than white, but I can promise you I know nothing more than the fact that the job was tendered for. There are people with far bigger stakes in Avalon who stand to make a lot more than I do, which, I must add, is a hell of a lot less than you think. If you think all of that money's going to go through the books, you need to think again.'

'How do you mean?' Culverhouse asked, his interest piqued.

'Listen, the money that's paid to Avalon is one thing. That's what'll be down on paper. But there's a whole lot more floating around in the darkness behind that. Legal fees, administration costs, consultancy services... All bywords they use to mask payments to interested parties. And besides, how difficult do you think it is to hide ten or twenty grand in cash in the middle of a multi-million pound development plan? I'll tell you — not very.'

Culverhouse leaned forward, meeting McCann's eyes. 'What are you saying? There are bungs involved?'

McCann laughed. 'If there's a council planning and development meeting, there's a brown envelope floating about. Trust me on that one. Nothing's completely above board with those bastards.'

'Hang on a sec,' said Culverhouse, frowning. 'Why are you telling me this? You're an Avalon shareholder. You make a nice bit of money out of every building contract they get. Why would you want to put that at risk by tipping me off about backroom deals?'

'Because, Detective Chief Inspector, it's those backroom deals that mean I'll be left with a lot less than you think I will. Sure, the development might be worth twenty mil. And seven percent of that is, what, almost one and a half mil. But I only get a dividend on profits. If that profit's all been eaten up by consultancy fees and administration charges that are being paid out to the main players, how much do you think I'll be left with? Believe me, I'm a minor player. I have no say in what Avalon do. And I definitely have no say in what happens to the hospital. That was decided a long time ago.'

'By who?'

'By the hospital trust and the council. If you want to find the really corrupt bastards, just look at them.'

44

'That doesn't really tell us a whole lot more than we already suspected,' Wendy said when Culverhouse told her about his visit to McCann's house.

'No, but it confirms it. And I know what you're going to say. You're going to say that we can't believe a bloody word he says. And usually you'd be right, but I saw it in his eyes. He's seriously fucked off about it as well. He knows he's owed more money than he's going to get out of this, and he knows it isn't the first time it's happened.'

Frank Vine laughed. 'Bloody hell. Gary McCann turns whistleblower. Never thought I'd see the day.'

'Oh, he's far from innocent, I'm sure. Might be worth us having a closer look at what else he's been up to. Feels like he opened up a little too easily for my liking.' Culverhouse paused for a moment, thinking. 'I wonder if he's preparing himself for a plea bargain, getting himself some brownie points.'

Before Culverhouse could say anything else, he was interrupted by his mobile phone ringing. Picking it up, he looked down at the display.

'Right. Knight, see what you can find out about the hospital trust. Who the directors are, the decision makers, all that. And find out who would've been the decision makers on the council's side. We need to do some digging into these bastards.'

Culverhouse walked into his office, closed the door behind him and pressed the *Answer* button.

'Helen,' he said, quietly.

'Jack. I got your message.'

He remembered leaving a long, rambling message a few nights ago after one too many whiskies, and he tried his hardest to remember what he'd said. 'Oh. Right.'

'Listen, you need to let this go, Jack. We both do. For our sakes and for Emily's.'

'I know. I just need to know where she is. I need to see her. It's... It's killing me.'

Helen was silent for a few moments. 'Jack, Emily isn't with me. She hasn't been for years.'

He swallowed. 'What? What do you mean?'

There was a brief pause, and then Helen spoke. 'When I left, it wasn't just because of you. It was because of me, too. I couldn't cope. Not with you, not with her. Not with life in general. When I left the house, I went straight to my parents. I told them... I told them some things that weren't strictly true. I shouldn't have done it, but it was the only way I could be free. For myself.'

Jack could feel his jaw clenching. *Try to stay calm. Don't lose your rag.* 'What did you tell them?'

'I told them you'd been abusive, that I felt scared and threatened. I knew they wouldn't be rushing to get in contact with you if I said that, and that if you came to them, they'd turn you away. They just wanted the best for me.'

He stayed silent for a few moments, trying to compose himself. It was an immensely hard thing to do. 'That's why they wouldn't take any of my calls. Why they said I shouldn't try to chase you.'

'Yes.'

'So when you left she was just thirty-five miles away?' He couldn't believe it, could hardly even get his head around this new piece of information. 'How long was she with them for?'

There was a pause. 'She's still with them, Jack.'

He could feel his heart thudding in his chest. All those years, all that time spent wondering where she was...

He took a deep breath before saying, 'I'm going over there.'

'No, you can't.'

'Try and stop me, Helen. I've waited long enough for this. I need—'

'No, I mean you can't because they've moved. They don't live in that house any more.'

'Where do they live?' he asked, calmly.

'Not far.'

He shook his head as he pressed his fingers into his eye

sockets, trying to push back the confusion. 'How the hell did you manage it? Thirty-five miles, for fuck's sake. How the hell did I not bump into her?'

'Because you didn't try to find her, Jack,' came the quiet reply. 'You didn't try. I knew that if you really wanted to, you could find her. And that if it got to that stage then you probably deserved to find her, because it would have shown that you actually, finally cared enough to go out of your way for us. But it took you eight and a half years, Jack. Why do you think I was so angry when I came back? What do you think it was like to find out how little you cared?'

He let out a huge breath. 'I did care, Helen. I *do*. I still do. Why do you think I've had people running around Spain trying to find you?'

'Listen,' Helen said, ignoring his question. 'Every Thursday and Friday she goes skateboarding at the skate park near where they live. She's there in the evenings, usually from about eight o'clock until ten. She'll be there tonight and tomorrow. Jack, don't go wading in. Please. But I know you want to see her, to see that she's alright. Promise me you'll keep your distance.'

He could feel his breath catching in his throat. He decided to say nothing about the fact that she was spending evenings out in a skate park on her own at her young age. He didn't know whether he wanted to laugh, cry, or be sick. Perhaps all three. 'How long ago did you last see her?' he asked, his voice almost cracking.

Helen was silent for a few moments. 'Too long.'

. . .

Once he'd managed to steel himself enough to leave his office and re-enter the major incident room, Culverhouse made his way across to the door on his unsteady legs, flinging the door open in his usual brash style.

'Right. Sorry about that,' he said, trying to sound as normal as possible. Where were we?'

'Mildenheath Hospital Trust,' Wendy said, standing in the middle of the room with a look on her face that said everything had changed. 'The board of directors. Three guesses as to who's the highest ranking medical specialist on the board, the person who'd have the most sway over the decision to close the hospital or not.'

'Go on.'

She sighed. 'One Julian Mills.'

45

'It seems pretty fucking clear to me,' Culverhouse said, the veins starting to appear across his forehead. 'You'd expect the senior consultants to be the ones who'd want the hospital to stay standing, so imagine the sway he'd have by speaking out in favour of knocking it down.'

'But it doesn't quite make sense,' Wendy said. 'Why would he? Like you said, you'd imagine that he'd be completely against the plans. He'd stand out like a sore thumb if he went against that stereotype.'

Culverhouse stood with his hands on his hips, trying to stop himself getting any angrier. 'He's a clever man, Knight. He knows that all he needs to do is admit to some of the benefits of merging care services, the cash-strapped NHS, all that bollocks. Or even just put forward arguments in favour of keeping the hospital open, while making those arguments majorly flawed, so they're shot down in flames by the "opposition". There are a hundred and one ways of doing it. It goes on all the time.'

'Why don't we have a closer look at his financial records?' Debbie Weston suggested.

'Worth a shot,' Wendy said, turning to her, 'but it's unlikely to show anything. This'll all be done under the radar somehow. Cash, gifts, favours in kind. They're not going to be that blatant about it, that's for sure.' She glanced at her watch. Shit. She hadn't realised how late it had got. Xav would be at the restaurant shortly.

'What about phone records? If we can find a direct link between Julian Mills and someone on the inside, that might open up a new line of enquiry.'

Steve Wing chipped in. 'But what would that actually prove? It just shows that he knows another bloke's phone number. What are we actually accusing him of?'

'Any number of things, Steve,' Culverhouse said, rounding on him. 'Corruption, illegal payments, potentially even fraud. Or how about that poor bloody woman lying in a coma in hospital?'

'We don't know he's involved in that, though,' Steve said, suddenly sounding unsure of himself.

'Oh come on, Steve. Join the dots. Julian Mills is on the board of directors for the Mildenheath Hospital Trust. The same hospital they're trying to get knocked down so they can build a housing estate worth twenty million quid. A housing estate that's being built by a company whose shareholders include the dodgiest fucker south of the North Pole. And this whole charade was being investigated by a woman who's randomly attacked — and almost murdered — on her own doorstep. Not only that, but she's currently in the loving care of the specialist brain injury unit at guess-which-hospital, being looked after by guess-which-consultant.'

'Yeah, and that's exactly what I mean,' Steve said, standing up. 'Isn't that all just a bit too convenient? Why have her put in that hospital? Why not just finish her off? Why hasn't he finished her off yet, if he's got all the means at his disposal?'

'Steve, look at the facts,' said Culverhouse. 'The attacker was disturbed. That's why Tanya Henderson didn't die. It's sheer luck — or bad luck, however you look at it — that it's her local hospital that has a specialist brain injury unit. But it's hardly a coincidence — it's the hospital Julian Mills works at, and the reason she discovered the whole scandal was because she lives locally, so she was bound to be sent there. I bet Mills thought all his Christmases had come at once when she got admitted.'

'And who was it who suggested putting her into an induced coma?' Wendy added. 'The nurse said herself that in her opinion, Tanya should've been kept out of a coma, or at least brought round sooner. With Tanya Henderson unconscious, he had her exactly where he needed her. Maybe he was planning to keep her in a coma until this whole deal had been signed off, I don't know. Maybe she was going to take an unfortunate turn for the worse in the middle of the night at some point. Maybe he was half banking on her waking up and not remembering a thing.

Who knows? He didn't plan it to work out this way, so he was playing it by ear as much as the rest were. And it's hardly surprising he re-induced the coma as soon as she started mumbling about Pevensey Park.'

'Would it be fair to say that you agree with me then, Detective Sergeant Knight?' Culverhouse asked, his hands still on his hips.

'Hey, I'm just throwing the theories out there. There's nothing we can prove,' replied Wendy, shrugging.

'No, but we don't have much choice, do we? Tanya Henderson is lying in that hospital bed being looked after by a man who's potentially involved in the reasons for her being there in the first place. If we're right, he'll want her dead.'

Wendy looked at her watch again. Xav would definitely be at the restaurant by now. He was always slightly early. 'Guv, I don't think you're wrong on this. Far from it. But we have a pretty major problem — there's no evidence. We can't just go wading in, throwing about accusations. And I'm sure Julian Mills won't just be taking bungs in his joint bank account. It'll be far more complex than that. We've got no way of proving it.'

Culverhouse smiled. 'We don't need to prove it.'

46

As far as Xav could tell, each of the songs being played in the restaurant sounded identical. They were all the same sort of traditional faux-Italian songs, middle-aged crooners singing the usual numbers: *Volare*; *Mambo Italiano*; *Arrivederci, Roma*. He tapped the bottom of his wine glass gently on the table in time to the music, watching the purplish liquid dance around the bowl of the glass, leaving a clear trail behind it.

He was only on his second glass of wine. The first had been because he was slightly nervous, plus he knew Wendy was likely to be late. She had a big case she was working on — that was fair enough — but dinner tonight had been her idea, and he had expected her to at least stick to that. Maybe he'd been right all along; maybe this wasn't something worth pursuing. But he'd bought the bottle of wine now, so he was going to at least give her the time that it took for him to drink it before he did anything daft.

A waiter floated over to the table. 'Can I get you anything at all, sir? Some bread and olives, perhaps?'

Xav went to wave him away, but then had a change of heart. 'Yeah, yeah some bread and olives would be lovely. Thanks.' He might as well get some food out of this, he thought.

He chastised himself for being too quick to jump to conclusions. She'd suggested the dinner, so there was no way she wasn't going to turn up. There might have been a breakthrough in the case, for all he knew. After all, some things were more important than dinner, but she only needed to let him know. Sure, he would've been disappointed — gutted, even — but at least he would have known, and he would have understood. Being sat on your own in a romantic restaurant was hardly a brilliant way to spend the evening, even if there was wine and food.

The waiter smiled at him as he placed the bread and olives on the table. It was a smile of pity, a smile that said *I'm sure she'll turn up soon* and *Let me know if you want to sneak out the fire door* at the same time.

The bread was still warm, and it smelled delicious. He took a bite, savouring the flavour, then washed it down with another mouthful of wine. If nothing else, he was enjoying the food and the drink, but he couldn't deny there was something missing.

He glanced at his watch. Eight-thirty. That was plenty late enough for him to be justified in calling her for an update, he thought. He took his phone out of his pocket and called her.

.   .   .

Wendy cursed at the unusually heavy traffic as she made her way along the high street, heading out of town towards the hospital. The roadworks for the new bypass were causing havoc in this area of town, especially when she really needed to get somewhere quickly. If Culverhouse had been here, he would've had the siren slapped on the roof and he'd be bombing down the wrong side of the road, overtaking the lot of them. But, being single-crewed and leading the way with Steve, Debbie, and Ryan in the car behind, she couldn't afford to be quite so maverick. However, a little bit of 'improvisation' wouldn't go amiss.

Approaching a roundabout, she got into the left-hand lane — a left-turn-only lane — and undertook a line of cars waiting patiently to enter the roundabout. Straddling the white lines, she managed to nip in front of a van that was going straight on, cutting into its lane and upsetting the driver, who responded with a long hard honk on the horn and a few choice hand gestures. Wendy raised her own hand in apology and kept her eyes on the road in front of her.

Her phone rang in the coin tray next to her and, glancing down, she could just about make out Xav's name flashing up on the screen.

'Damnit, Xav,' she said to herself, knowing she couldn't answer while she was driving. The hospital was only a mile away now. She'd call him when she got there.

.   .   .

After the seventh or eighth ring, the call went through to voicemail. He had no intention of leaving a voicemail. After all, what would he say? If she wasn't here, she wasn't here. She couldn't enjoy the ambience or eat a meal through her answerphone.

He didn't know whether to feel angry or disappointed. He felt a mixture of both.

He'd heard it a number of times — don't get into a relationship with a police officer. And although he'd always known what they meant, he'd also hoped it wouldn't matter. He thought things might be different with him, different with Wendy. In many ways, she wasn't the same as a lot of the others. But in some ways, it seemed, she was.

'Any luck?' the waiter said, approaching his table.

Xav looked down at his phone.

'No. No luck.'

47

Jack Culverhouse had his pedal to the metal, too, although he wasn't heading in the direction of Mildenheath Hospital. He'd told the others he wanted to head over on his own as he had to quickly do something first. Once they'd left, he'd got in his car and started off towards the town Helen's parents lived in.

The drive seemed to happen on autopilot, a thousand and one thoughts flitting around in his head as he tried to keep his emotions in check. There was still something at the back of his mind that told him this wasn't really happening, that Helen had lied again or fed him another red herring, but none of that mattered. All that mattered was that there was a possibility, a small chance, a tiny ray of hope. If he was willing to get on a flight to Spain because someone he'd never heard of reckoned he'd spotted someone who might have looked a bit like Emily, then he was perfectly happy to make the short drive up the road to a skate park.

His sat nav told him there were just two miles to go, and he could feel his heart rate increasing every time that distance dropped. 1.9 miles. 1.8. 1.7. He could feel his love for his daughter growing the closer he got. In that regard, time hadn't changed a thing.

He hadn't thought about what he was going to say; he didn't even know if he was going to say anything. He might just park up and watch, see if it was her. He didn't know what he was going to do if it was. He'd just play it by ear. Sometimes things are better left unplanned. After all, a parent knows instinctively what to do at times of stress. It's an inbuilt, ingrained ability.

As the miles remaining turned into yards, Jack felt his knees quivering with every gear change, his leg starting to shake as he applied the brake and pulled over into a parking bay near the skate park.

He could just about see people in there, skating, but while it was floodlit, it was still impossible to see anything at this distance.

Opening the car door, he got out, the fresh air hitting him like a ton of bricks. He suddenly felt very queasy, but he managed to just about hold it in. His legs struggling to carry him, he made his way over to the line of trees that surrounded three sides of the skatepark, locking the car behind him.

The trees were fairly new, as was the skatepark, so they provided decent cover whilst still allowing him to see through. As he got closer, he began to walk more slowly, mentally discounting the skaters one by one as he saw them. Most of them were boys. Four of them were skating, one with his long hair tucked under a beanie cap, turning a kick flip on the halfpipe as Culverhouse watched him soar gracefully through the air.

And that's when he saw her.

She couldn't have looked any more different from the girl he remembered. Her hair was dark now, almost black, and the amount of makeup she was wearing — visible even at this distance — made her look as if she was at least eighteen. The cute little girl in pigtails was gone, replaced by a dress code Jack could only describe as something in between gothic and burlesque.

She rested her head on the shoulder of the boy next to her, a boy who looked much older than she was, and who had his arm around her, his hand resting on her knee.

Jack got closer, and before he realised it he'd entered the skatepark and was walking over towards her.

The closer he got, the more certain he was. It was her. Even with all the time that had passed, he would still have recognised her a mile off. There was no way he couldn't have.

He was now maybe fifty feet away, and he felt sure she'd look up and see him soon.

His legs turned to jelly again, and he stopped walking, breathing deeply and trying to control his heart rate.

He called out. 'Emily?'

She looked up, the smile dropping from her face as she

saw him. She stared for a few moments, whispered some-thing to her boyfriend, then stood up, walking over to him with purpose.

Another boy called out from the left, 'You alright, Jet?'

She raised a hand to him, as if to tell him she had it all under control.

Jack was speaking before he'd even realised he'd opened his mouth. 'Jet? Who's Jet?'

When she was about twenty feet away, she slowed, as if she couldn't bring herself to move any closer.

Culverhouse stared at her, now completely unable to speak.

'Dad? What the fuck are you doing here?'

48

Wendy walked onto the ward alone, asking the nurse at the desk if she could see Julian Mills.

'Yeah, I think he's still here,' the nurse said. Wendy didn't doubt it. 'I'll just check for you.'

Wendy thanked her and sat down on one of the chairs, looking again at her watch. She knew she ought to call Xav back, or at least fire him a quick text, but by now she was almost three quarters of an hour late and whatever she said wasn't going to do any good. She would just have to grovel again tomorrow. She convinced herself he'd understand.

Steve, Debbie and Ryan were all waiting exactly where she'd asked them to wait — or where Culverhouse had asked them to wait, anyway. After all, this was meant to be his operation, and he was meant to have met them here. Steve had received an odd call from him shortly after they'd left, telling him he wouldn't be going over to the hospital as he had to be elsewhere. Something more important had come up, he'd said.

Still thinking about Xav, Wendy changed her mind and decided to send him a text — just a quick update to apologise profusely and to let him know she'd explain all tomorrow. Before she could, however, the familiar but charming voice of Julian Mills came echoing down the corridor.

'Detective Sergeant Knight, you're working late.'

'Overtime,' she replied. 'Comes in handy sometimes.'

'I bet. So what can I do for you?'

'I was just wondering if I might be able to ask you a few questions. Can we?' she said, gesturing to the private room beside them.

Julian Mills nodded, and they entered.

'Firstly, do you have any idea what Tanya Henderson meant when she said "Pevensey Park"?'

His facial expression looked well-rehearsed; almost too perfect. 'Pevensey Park?' he repeated.

'Yes. We were told that just before she was put back into an induced coma, she said the words "Pevensey Park" a few times over. Do you know what they mean?'

'No, I'm afraid not. Should I?'

Wendy broke eye contact with Mills as she said, 'I'll get straight to the point. Where were you on the night Tanya Henderson was attacked?' It was a far more direct approach than she'd use in any other situation, but she had her reasons.

'Me? Well, I was here, working.'

'What time did you sign in?'

'About six o'clock that evening. I was rostered on until six the next morning.'

'And did you leave the hospital at all during your shift?'

'No, not at all. I barely leave the ward. We don't exactly get lunch breaks in this job, you know.'

Wendy nodded, looking at him again. 'And what do you know about the plans to close this hospital and build a housing estate on the land?'

Julian Mills smiled, before letting out a nervous laugh. 'What is this? Are you accusing me of something?'

'Just answer the question please, Mr Mills.'

He sighed, rubbing his chin before speaking. 'I'm on the board for the hospital trust. Our job is to discuss the future of the hospital and decide on strategies for saving money and delivering the best possible patient care.' It sounded like a well-rehearsed line, almost a sales pitch.

'In which case you'll be able to tell me all about the plans, won't you?' Wendy said, as politely as she could.

Mills sat down on the arm of a chair, looking up at her. It seemed like a well-rehearsed piece of body language too: get lower, make the other person feel like they're in control. 'What more do you want me to say? Like all hospitals, we're struggling for funding, and there is a proposal on the table for merging primary care treatments into other local hospitals to make sure we can keep treating patients to a high standard during difficult times.'

'Because of the shortage of money?'

'Indeed.'

'And how much money do you stand to make from the sale of the hospital?' Wendy asked.

Mills laughed; a deep, guttural belly laugh. 'Me? Absolutely nothing. This may come as a surprise to you, but I don't own the hospital. I'm simply one of the appointed officials who helps decide its future.'

Wendy nodded. 'So you're not in receipt of any financial benefits or payments which might have influenced your decision at all?'

The consultant's eyes narrowed. 'Are you accusing me of corruption, Detective Sergeant Knight? Because that's a very serious allegation.'

'I'm simply asking questions, Mr Mills. That's my job.'

'And my job is to help steer the future of this hospital and ensure the best possible treatment for our patients, whatever the means to that end may be.'

To Wendy, Julian Mills had the patter of an experienced politician — and he was just as slippery and evasive, too. That relaxed Scottish charm had suddenly begun to seem very sinister indeed, and she started to feel rather uncomfortable in his presence.

'Thank you, Mr Mills. I'm sure we'll be in touch very soon,' she said, holding eye contact for longer than was necessary, and far longer than she felt comfortable with.

Leaving the room, she headed back down the corridor before pressing the button for the lift. She couldn't wait to get out of there.

. . .

Julian Mills looked out of the window, watching the police-woman make her way across the car park towards her car. He didn't quite know what she was playing at, but he knew the net was closing. If he was going to be caught, however, he was going to make sure he went down fighting.

Everything was coincidental. Everything was pure conjecture. There was nothing they could prove, else he'd be walking across that car park with her, in handcuffs. And there was only one way they were going to be able to obtain any evidence. If that source of evidence were gone...

In that moment, he knew that control was fully in his hands. And he knew exactly how to exercise it.

49

You'd imagine that calmness and confusion wouldn't go together very well, but they're doing a very good job of cancelling each other out. My body is relaxed, yet my mind is screaming; the desperation to yell out is being quashed by the calmness I know is being provided by the drugs. Black and white. Yin and yang.

It's a terrifying position to be in, feeling completely in control of your mind but unable to do a thing about your body. That control has been hard fought, but I've got there. I've gradually learned to separate the wheat from the chaff, work through my memories, understand the stimuli. What else is there to do when you're lying in a hospital bed, unable to move? If you do nothing, you'll go mad.

All I can do is hope. Hope that the words I thought I was saying actually got out; hope that they got to the right people; hope that those people know what to do about them.

But I've got time on my side, haven't I? There's a police

presence on the ward. They can't do anything while the police are here. Can they?

I know I'm unlikely to get another chance to speak out. They're not going to give me a second opportunity. I just need to pray with every fibre of my being that I made the most of my first.

There's a good chance it's too late. I know that. And a kind of grudging yet peaceful acceptance is washing over me. When you know there's truly nothing you can do, the human brain has a marvellous way of ridding itself of all worry. After all, what's the point? Que sera, sera.

And it's then that I realise why I've reached this level of acceptance, why I've made peace with myself and my situation. It's because I know it's too late. I hear the footsteps. I recognise them immediately. No-one else wears hard soles on this ward. No-one else walks with that particular gait, that pattern of moving.

And again, I feel my mind detach from my body. It's as if I'm floating, up above myself, watching on as a spectator as I see myself lying in the hospital bed with him standing over me. And I watch as he loosens a tube, detaches a wire. I see the monitor start to change its display, warning that things aren't going quite right.

And everything starts to become very dark.

50

Julian Mills stood in Tanya Henderson's room on the ward, watching the monitor next to her bed. Her breathing had become laboured without the endotracheal tube, which lay on the pillow next to her head, the bulbous end thick with a coating of mucus and saliva.

He could feel his heart beating in his chest, knowing it wouldn't be long until it happened. And he had to hope that the nurse wouldn't arrive in the meantime.

The bleeping of the monitoring equipment was far louder than he wanted it to be, and he was pleased that he'd asked the nurse to fetch him something from the café while he watched the fort. Sure, she'd think him a complete sexist arsehole, but so what? At least she wouldn't know the real truth. And even if she did, it would never be proven.

Once it was too late — once Tanya's heart had stopped beating for a minute or so — he'd reinsert the breathing tube and reattach the monitoring equipment. Her lungs would fill with air and empty, over and over again, but it would be no use. The monitoring equipment would detect no pulse. And he'd be back at the reception, assiduously keeping an eye on the desk, just like he said he would.

Only a couple of seconds had passed, but it felt like much longer. Fortunately, he'd timed the walk to and from the café himself. If you took the stairs it was a round trip of eight minutes, thirty seconds. If you took the lift it could be anywhere between eight and nine minutes. Factor in the time it'd take her to find what he wanted and buy it, and you were probably looking at a safe nine minutes, possibly ten. He'd be out of here within eight anyway, if only this bloody woman would die.

This bloody woman who'd tried to ruin his life, who'd been sniffing around and asking too many questions. And now look at what she was making him do. This went against everything he knew, everything he'd trained his whole life to do. His Hippocratic Oath, gone up in flames. He'd never wanted it to come to this. That was why he'd hired Clyde in the first place. He was meant to do the dirty work, keeping him one step removed. Clyde would have been paid pretty handsomely, too — a small cut of the money Mills was due to get from the deal, but still a decent amount. But he'd fucked it up. He'd have to deal with him later. Calmly, of course. Anything else just wouldn't do. Pay him off, keep him quiet. He might have fucked it up, but there was a whole lot more he could fuck up if he wanted to.

Mills fixed his eyes on the woman in the bed. He could swear her face contorted slightly as she struggled and fought for her last breath, though he knew it couldn't be possible. She was far too unconscious. It wouldn't even be instant rigor, the state in which a body enters rigor mortis at the moment it expires, usually when there's an intense struggle and a large amount of physical exertion as they die. Tanya Henderson's muscles, however, would be as relaxed as they could be. Too relaxed, in fact, which was why she needed the endotracheal tube in order to breathe.

Barely ten seconds had passed. Eight minutes was going to feel like an age. Everything seemed to slow down in front of him, including the slight movement of the floor-length curtains, which twitched and twisted momentarily just before he felt the hand clamp down on his right shoulder.

The blood pulsed in his ears, a deep, throbbing sound, as a woman, slight and slender, stepped out from behind the curtain. He turned to see who had their hand on his shoulder — strong and firm — and as he did so he saw the blue blur of the nurse's uniform as she rushed past him to Tanya's bed.

The sounds rushed back into his ears, time sped back up, and he started to feel extremely dizzy and sick. Coloured spots began to appear in his vision, the edges fading to blackness. The last thing he heard before his legs buckled and he passed out were some words about anything he said being used as evidence.

51

They say any good plan needs extensive planning and immaculate execution. This one hadn't been long in the planning stage at all, but the execution had been textbook.

Wendy knew that her direct line of questioning would've forced Julian Mills's hand. Mills knew that if they got into a position where they could arrest him on suspicion of anything, someone else would have been put in charge of Tanya Henderson's medical care and she'd be taken out of the coma in no time. Then the only witness, the only person who knew what had really happened, would be there to tell her tale. Wendy knew that Mills would only be left with one option — to finish Tanya off there and then.

Everyone knew their roles, and they'd executed them to perfection. Shortly after Wendy and Julian Mills had gone into the side room to talk, Steve, Debbie and Ryan had entered the ward. Debbie had informed the nurse of what was happening, Ryan had positioned herself behind the curtain in Tanya's room and Steve had lain in wait inside a store cupboard, ready to apprehend Mills and make the arrest once he'd been seen removing the monitoring equipment and breathing tube.

A fresh-faced and inexperienced lawyer might try to claim entrapment, but they'd been very careful. They hadn't led him to commit a crime — they'd simply opened up the opportunity and watched him take it. And he'd acted exactly as they'd hoped he would.

Fortunately for them, Julian Mills had acted not like a hardened, always-suspicious criminal, but like the desperate and hopeless man that he was.

Mills had regained consciousness a couple of minutes later. It hadn't been anything serious — just the pure shock and realisation of what was happening. After a couple of glasses of water and a journey back to Mildenheath Police Station in the back of the car, he'd been booked in and had his lawyer called for him.

The lawyer looked completely out of his depth, and Wendy guessed that this probably wasn't his particular area of expertise. Jack Culverhouse didn't appear to be on his finest form either, having suddenly reappeared half an hour earlier looking as though he'd just watched all the *Saw* films back to back after a heavy meal.

'Do we really need to be doing this at this time of night?' the lawyer asked as they entered the interview room, looking as though he'd much rather be in bed.

'Yes, we do. Time is of the essence,' Culverhouse said,

referring to the fact that they would have just twenty-four hours to interview him and build a case strong enough to convince the Crown Prosecution Service to let them charge him.

Wendy started the interview, getting Julian Mills to confirm his name and address. This was the first time he'd spoken since the moment of his arrest — he'd been completely silent otherwise.

'Julian, can you tell me what your connection was to Tanya Henderson?'

'You don't need to say anything. You can say "no comment" if you like,' his lawyer said.

Julian Mills sighed. 'More recently she was my patient, but before that she was the journalist investigating the Pevensey Park development plans.'

'Julian, you don't need to say any of this,' the lawyer repeated, now looking even more concerned.

'I want to. I need to,' he replied. 'She'd been sniffing around and asking questions, and when I looked into her history and the things she'd done before — the people she'd exposed, the lives she'd ruined — I knew something had to be done. I had too much to lose.'

'And anything to gain?' Wendy asked.

'Yes. A lot. Enough to retire more than comfortably. And all I had to do was to try and put forward a positive case for merging the hospital services and closing Mildenheath. As simple as that.'

'Who asked you to do it?' Culverhouse asked.

Julian Mills didn't reply.

'Was it Gary McCann?'

Mills's eyes narrowed. 'Who?'

Culverhouse could see instantly that he'd never heard of McCann. 'He's a shareholder in Avalon Construction. He lives locally.'

'Oh. No, I don't know him. I think there's quite a few people involved with Avalon.'

'Who was your contact? Who was paying you?' Culverhouse tried asking again.

Mills sighed, louder this time. 'Can we talk about that side of things later?'

'If you like,' Culverhouse replied. 'And what about Callum Woods?' he asked, watching Mills's eyes for a flicker of recognition. There was nothing.

'Who?'

'Callum Woods. He'd been a previous and present customer of Avalon and had been a target of Tanya Henderson's a year or so ago.'

'Oh. Yes I know now. The footballer?'

'That's him,' Culverhouse said. 'What was his involvement?'

Mills curled his bottom lip and shook his head. 'Nothing as far as I know. But then I don't know who was meant to be involved. They kind of kept me on the sidelines.'

'So when Tanya Henderson ended up on your ward, was that by accident or design?' Wendy asked.

'Bit of both, I guess. She wasn't meant to end up in hospital at all. She was meant to die. But when she didn't, and with her brain injury, well... I stepped in. It's my specialist area.'

At the word 'die', Mills's lawyer lowered his head. He didn't look happy.

'Handy,' Wendy said, almost sarcastically.

Julian Mills didn't reply.

'And what was the plan?' she asked. 'When she didn't die but was lying in a hospital bed on your ward. What were your intentions?'

Shaking his head, Mills looked at the floor. 'I don't know. I didn't know what to think or what to do. But she was there, in my ward, effectively under my control. The induced coma meant that I could keep an eye on her. It gave me time to work out what I was going to do.'

'And when you did bring her out of her coma, presumably so the eyes of suspicion didn't fall on you for keeping her in it in the first place, she started talking about Pevensey Park.'

Mills spoke quietly. 'Yes. And that's when I knew I only had one option.'

Wendy could sense that Culverhouse's patience was wearing thin as he asked him forcefully, 'Why are you telling us this, Mills? It's a pretty extraordinary confession.'

'I'm not a career criminal, Inspector. I'm a medical professional. I did a very stupid thing. And now I need to make amends.'

Wendy raised an eyebrow. She still wasn't entirely sure

Julian Mills realised the gravity of what he'd done, or the charges he was facing, but even if he didn't, at least he was talking. That was the main thing.

And Wendy was growing increasingly confident that he'd be brought to justice for the crimes he'd committed.

There was always a strange lull after a big case, almost as if handing it over to the Crown Prosecution Service left a vacuum. It was a vacuum that Wendy liked to fill with a bottle of wine.

She still felt incredibly guilty for not letting Xav know she wouldn't be able to make it to the meal. She felt even worse for not having texted or called him since.

It had been a mad twenty-four hours. One moment she'd been about to leave and head home, ready to prepare herself for the meal with Xav, and before she knew it, everything had changed. They'd apprehended and arrested Mills, conducted the interviews overnight and through the next day and had compiled a case that even the CPS couldn't deny. She'd just about managed to snatch a couple of hours' sleep late morning, which had resulted in her feeling both absolutely knackered but also unable to get to sleep now that evening had come around again.

She picked up her phone and called Xav, knowing that he'd definitely be home from work by now.

The phone rang six or seven times, then went through to voicemail.

She gave it a few minutes, then tried again. She got the same result.

Xav never let his phone go through to voicemail. He always answered somehow.

She opened up her *Messages* app and typed out a text to him, apologising and trying, poorly, to explain what had happened. As she sent the text message, the word *Delivered* appeared underneath it. A few seconds later, it changed to *Read 19:49*. She knew that as soon as he started typing a reply, three dancing dots would appear on the screen.

There were none.

Jack sat in his armchair, his eyes glazing over as he stared at the TV. He wasn't even sure what was on — something about street markets in China from what he could make out, but he wasn't really watching.

A glass of whisky sat on the table in front of him, as yet untouched.

There was far too much going on in his mind to be able to relax. The closure of the Tanya Henderson case had been one thing, but coming at the same time as he'd finally managed to track down Emily, just a few miles away, had really taken it out of him.

He rubbed his hand across his stubbled chin, a couple of days' growth now apparent, and sighed.

Beside him on the armchair, his mobile phone vibrated. It was a text message, one from a number he didn't recognise.

He knew immediately who it was. He'd given her his number, asked her to contact him if she had even the slightest desire to get to know him, if there was even the smallest hint that she might be able to forgive him and try to work at rebuilding. She hadn't seemed keen at the time — not at all — but now he was starting to think otherwise.

Taking a deep breath, he unlocked his phone and read the message.

Dad, it's me. Can we talk?

GET MORE OF MY BOOKS FREE!

Thank you for reading *In Too Deep*. I hope it was as much fun for you as it was for me writing it.

To say thank you, I'd like to invite you to my exclusive *VIP Club*, and give you some of my books and short stories for FREE. All members of my VIP Club have access to FREE, exclusive books and short stories which aren't available anywhere else.

You'll also get access to all of my new releases at a bargain-basement price before they're available anywhere else. Joining is absolutely FREE and you can leave at any time, no questions asked. To join the club, head to adamcroft.net/vip-club **and two free books will be sent to you straight away!**

If you enjoyed the book, please do leave a review on

the site you bought it from. Reviews mean an awful lot to writers and they help us to find new readers more than almost anything else. It would be very much appreciated.

I love hearing from my readers, too, so please do feel free to get in touch with me. You can contact me via my website, on Twitter @adamcroft and you can 'like' my Facebook page at facebook.com/adamcroftbooks.

For more information, visit my website: adamcroft.net

An anonymous phone call reveals a horrifying secret. But can it be murder if there isn't a body?

Father Joseph Kümmel is not just a deeply religious and spiritual man. He's the leader of a closed religious community at Hilltop Farm — one which kills members who want to leave.

When someone manages to get messages to DCI Jack Culverhouse and DS Wendy Knight about the goings-on at Hilltop Farm, they begin to uncover a web of dark deception and murderous intent. With a distinct lack of evidence and a community distrustful of the police, they're left fighting against the odds.

The stakes are raised when their attempts to charge Father Joseph are blocked by higher powers. Will they be able to uncover the truth in time to stop his plans for a far more sinister fate for the residents of Hilltop Farm?

Turn the page to read the first chapter...

IN THE NAME OF THE FATHER

CHAPTER 1

Isabella Martin stood rooted to the spot as Father Joseph Kümmel's eyes bore into hers. For a while, he said no words. He didn't need to.

She'd been considering her escape from Hilltop Farm for some time. Recently she'd made the grave mistake of voicing her doubts to another member of the community. She'd thought she could trust her, considered her a friend. But now she was standing in front of the man who'd started this, who'd brought them all here, and expected her to repent for her sins.

'Isabella, do you ever plan your own death?' the man said, his deep Germanic tones rumbling as he spoke.

The farmhouse smelt damp and musty, as it always did at this time of year. The room felt oppressive, little light sneaking in through the small, high windows. Although she stood alone, facing the seated Father Joseph across his desk, she felt a thousand eyes upon her. The building was known as the chapel, although Isabella had long since rejected it as such in her mind. To her, it was now just another farmhouse. In any case, it felt more like a crypt than a chapel.

She swallowed, her mouth dry, struggling for something to say.

'No... No, I don't.'

Father Joseph smiled. It wasn't a happy smile, but the knowing twinkle of a parent whose child has just told them they're going to be an astronaut when they grow up.

'Do you not find that odd? After all, let's face it: you're going to die. We all are. Do you not think it important to plan ahead and take control over that event?'

Isabella clenched her teeth. Control was something she'd lacked for a long time, something she'd gradually come to realise she was missing. And here was the man she held responsible, urging her to take control, telling her it was within her power. Had she been wrong all along? Had Father Joseph been guiding her nobly, the only resistance coming from within herself?

'It... It's not something I've ever thought about,' she said, desperate to gauge Father Joseph's mood and thoughts from the look in his eyes.

'Do you not think it is time to think about it?' he said, cocking his head slightly to one side. He stayed silent, looking at her. Isabella could tell he was going to say no more and felt compelled to speak next.

'I'm not sure what you mean.'

Father Joseph smiled again.

'Child, you have a strong character. A strength of will. It is that strength of will that compelled you to express your doubts, to consider leaving the community. Do you see now that you were misguided in that sentiment?'

Isabella nodded, unable to express any words. She tried to work out whether he was angry or empathetic, but couldn't.

'You are not to blame, Isabella,' he said, as if reading her mind and wanting to answer her question. 'It is perfectly natural for someone as strong willed as you to doubt. But you are also well aware of what dark forces have planted that doubt, are you not?'

She nodded again. The word wasn't one that was ever spoken within the community. No matter how removed Isabella had felt from this place recently, she still felt a cold shiver down her spine whenever she even considered it.

'Which is why it is time for you to take control, Isabella. You are in charge of your own destiny. You make every decision in your life through free will. It is your free will that brought you here, that put you under the wing of God's love. You are a person in control. Do you want those dark forces to consume you from within, to take that control away from you?'

Isabella shook her head, slowly at first.

'No... No.'

'Then you must take the ultimate control,' he said, sliding a coffee mug across the desk towards her with the tips of his fingers. 'You must make the decision. Take the

step that most people will never have the strength of character to take.'

Isabella looked down at the coffee mug. It looked like
any cup of coffee, except there was no steam. She looked
back up at Father Joseph, seeing that his eyes had never
left hers.

'I... I can't,' she said. 'I don't want to.'

'It is not you speaking, Isabella. You want to take
control. You want to make this choice.'

'No... No. I don't. I can't,' she said, her voice faltering.

Father Joseph clenched his jaw. Isabella heard two
footsteps to her side. She turned her head and saw the faint
but familiar frame of Nelson, one of Father Joseph's closest
confidants. His eyes were milky and tense, his black skin
still disguised in the shadows. She caught a glint of light
that flashed below and just to the left of Nelson. It was
only for a moment, but enough to make her realise that he
was holding a gun in his right hand.

Isabella looked back at the coffee mug.

She recalled the stories one of the other members of
the community had told her. Legend was that those who
transgress are sometimes made to prove their devotion to
the community and to Father Joseph. Long before Isabella
had come to the farm, a male member of the community
was apparently handed a gun by Father Joseph and told to
kill one of the two of them. The man had lifted the gun to
his own temple and pulled the trigger, only to find the gun
hadn't been loaded. From that point on, having proven his
devotion, the man had lived the life of a king. Isabella

didn't know his name, or what had ultimately happened to him, nor did she know anyone who'd ever met him. But the story remained powerful, indelible on her consciousness.

Was this what was happening here? Was this simply a harmless mug of cold coffee, intended to be a make-or-break moment for her? Either way, she now knew what the alternative was. She glanced back at Nelson, herself almost able to feel the cold steel of the gun.

She extended her arm, her elbow popping as she did so, and took hold of the coffee cup. Slowly, she lifted it to her lips and drank.

It was definitely coffee, she knew that much. Cold coffee. Knowing the taste would be unpleasant, and only wanting to experience it once, she slugged back the mug's contents in one.

Within seconds of putting the mug down, she could feel the butterflies in her chest and throat. Her neck tightened as she began to gasp for breath. Time seemed to slow, her legs buckling from under her as her stomach began to heave, her body shivering as it began to convulse. Without warning, she vomited, the stream of liquid splattering across the concrete floor of the farmhouse, masking the sound of her losing control of her bowel and bladder.

Gradually, everything faded, became black.

Want to read on?

Visit adamcroft.net/book/in-the-name-of-the-father/ to grab your copy.

ACKNOWLEDGMENTS

As with all of my books, I have a number of people to thank for getting it to this stage. Primarily, though, my thanks must go to you, the reader, for buying and reading this book.

To Dr John Lloyd, for helping me find information on brain injuries and head trauma.

To the forty-four people who rallied around and suggested kids' TV programmes when I put out a request on Facebook. You should all have better things to do.

To my editor, Jessica Coleman, for her sterling work once again.

To Lucy Hayward, my Queen Beta Reader, who knows my books better than I do.

To all of the members of my VIP Club, now tens of thousands strong, whom I value immeasurably.

To everyone who's got in touch over the past few

months with lovely emails, tweets, Facebook messages and even comments in the street. It's been a remarkable year.

Printed in April 2022
by Rotomail Italia S.p.A., Vignate (MI) - Italy